# Snow Black, The Seven
## Stori

To.

Barbara

with Love

Talisha x

17. 06. 10

# SNOW BLACK,

# THE SEVEN RASTAS

# &

## OTHER SHORT STORIES

By
Talisha Cree Johnson

Illustrations by Dee Lewars

**Grafted**

Published in Great Britain by **Grafted**

www.graftedbydesign.co.uk

ISBN: 978-0-9562603-4-5

# FOREWORD

We talk a lot these days of engaging young people and making things relevant. This is a book written by a young person that will instantly engage and speak to young people and adults alike. Talisha Johnson, herself, is 16 and currently one of the Head girls at Great Barr School, Birmingham. She is an exemplary pupil who in the future would like to study journalism at university.

You will find this book as varied as it is creative. It contains seven short stories which are completely different to each other; some appeal to the imagination and are the 21$^{st}$ century equivalent of 'Alice in Wonderland'; others will get you tingling all over with excitement and anticipation. My favourite is definitely 'Snow Black and The Seven Rastas for its perceptions and humour. Talisha attributes her creative writing gifts to God but I know that she has also benefited from the inspiration of her mother who has been writing poetry from an early age and published her own book a couple of years ago entitled 'My Lover, My King & I'.

This book is an excellent accomplishment and I hope it will be used in the curriculum of many schools.

Sheila Hendley – Director of Academy for Life.

# Dedication

Firstly, I thank God for giving me this wonderful opportunity to make this dream a reality.

Secondly, to the best parents in the world Dennis and Esha Johnson who have always told me 'I can'.

Thirdly, Mrs Ferreira, my Year 9 English teacher, who refused to accept my second best and extracted the A star pupil in me.

To family, friends and everyone who has supported and encouraged me to write this book.

Most importantly, to all young people and anyone with dreams and the desire to write.

# Preface

Writing, to me, is more than fancy words written on a page, it's a creative part of life. It allows me to express, imagine and explore, enabling my mind to think beyond the human mind-set and allowing it to venture out to reach the unthinkable.

My mum encouraged me to keep a journal from the age of five years old. This was the start of developing my passion for writing. At the age of eleven years I had an overwhelming desire to write a book but felt this was out of my depth. Somehow I believed that this was an area for experienced authors who were already established in their work e.g. Jacqueline Wilson, Malorie Blackman, Sharon G. Flake. After all, I was only a child with a dream. I asked myself the question who would want to read my book? If they did, how do I begin? Where do I start? Fortunately for me I have the most incredible parents who believe that dreams are possible. They encouraged me to rise to the challenge and follow the desire of my heart. My parents would tell me about people like Sir Richard Branson who refused to give up on his dream when others told him he would never make it. Where there is passion there is a way.

I have written this book not only to fulfil my own dream but to encourage and inspire all young people to go ahead and fulfil their true potential. I believe every young person is designed for greatness. We are all unique in our own way. We all have something to offer. Most young people think they should wait to reach the years of adulthood to accomplish their goal; but this is simply not true, I wrote this book at the age of 15.

I implore all young people to follow their heart's desires especially those who write creatively like myself, it is the best decision you could ever make in your life. Remember! 'Can't' means shan't and won't; *I 'Can'* **gives you the ability to succeed.** It's not too late to be the best you that you can be.

# Contents

# CLAIRE'S MYSTERY

Back at home

Silence drowned the entire atmosphere of the house. Faces were blank and voices didn't utter a word. It had been two weeks since their daughter Claire had died, and the reality of the whole situation still hadn't sunk in. The house had come to a complete standstill. It was a great shock that was clearly unexpected. Family and friends had gathered with cards and flowers, all on their way to place them at the crime scene where she was found. Grandma Wendy-May did her best to keep everything and everyone in order; it was the only thing she could do, well, to detract her attention from thinking about her beloved, precious granddaughter.

Simon, Claire's dad sat with his head resting in the white disfigured shape of his unsettling palm. He was a tall, strapping fellow, a dark brunette with hazel eyes; hazel eyes that were now filled with sleepless nights, tears and sorrow. As for her mum, Yvonne, she had dropped 2 stone and had returned to that awful habit of smoking again, which Claire oh so despised! Her skin was pale and lifeless with eyes drooped like railings of curtains and black mascara smeared across her eyelids. She looked like a twig on legs, with bones popping out of her chest; it was an awful sight to bear. Simon glared at the cigarette scornfully, as he despised it just as much as his daughter did. Rising to his feet, he was quick but also extremely careful whilst taking it out of Yvonne's quivering hand, he then casually placed his arm around her shoulder.

"Everything will be OK, love," he whispered gently into her small, dainty ear. Her face rose for their eyes to meet and bursting into a great flood of tears she buried her head into his broad shoulder.

"I want Claire! I want my little girl back!" she screamed helplessly at the top of her lungs, drawing everyone's attention to her. Simon tried to hush her in a calm and collective manner.

"Don't touch me!" she scowled at him.

Leaving him hurt and embarrassed, with a strong mighty force, she untangled herself from his grip and ran out of the living room with her hands clasped over her pink face. A pink vulnerable face, drowned heavily in endless teardrops. She ran and ran, across the hallway, up the stairs, across the landing and then she stopped. Something had drawn her hasty actions to an immediate halt, taking a deep breath and a step back; she had brought herself to take the first step into Claire's bedroom since she was *taken*.

Everything was in its rightful place, jeans on the floor, tops flung over the sides of the wardrobe, dressing table full of cosmetics, an unmade bed full of clean and dirty underwear. Last but not least, Jimmy, Claire's *'I can't possibly live without you'* purple teddy bear. It was given to her at the age of 7 months and had never left her bedside. The 'perfect' bedroom she'd call it if she were there. Yes, *everything* just the way Claire liked it. Yvonne smiled gently wiping a great mass of green mucus from her runny nose.

"She was just your typical, ordinary teenager," she said in a calm, relaxing tone. Placing herself on the untidy bed, her hand reached for Jimmy. She ran her fingers through his fluffy, smooth purple skin stroking it slowly. Her nose then rested in his head sniffing the very intense aroma of his being. As she did this, she rocked him gently at a rhythm-based pace.

It was in that particular quiet time, that she had spent a while in Claire's room alone, that she began to reminisce about the short life of her daughter. The life that was unfairly cut short with no explanation.

"Is there any justice in this world for a mother like me? Can anybody hear me up there? Is there anybody who even cares?" Yvonne questioned, and questioned life itself until reducing herself to more outrageous cries. She couldn't possibly contain it. It just kept on coming and gushing out like a boisterous waterfall.

Her mind then began to wonder, wondering where and what Claire might be doing at this present moment in time. Was she happy wherever she was now? Was she sad? Was she being looked after by somebody else up there? A firm knock at the door alerted her attention instantly.

"I want to be left alone," she demanded in a monotonous tone, whilst coming out of her train of thoughts.

"Yvonne love, it's me, can I come in?"
Simon then lowered his voice even more, and repeated the question. He sensed her hostility strongly and was more mindful this time round not to upset her again. As he finally took the hint that his wife wasn't going to respond or acknowledge his presence, he entered the room on his own account. He joined her where she was seated on Claire's bed. His attention was drawn straight to Jimmy who was still placed in her arms.

"Jimmy," Simon chuckled, as if trying to engage in casual conversation.
He then pulled her close, kissing the side of her wet cheek. His grip was tight and firmly secure, as if to make sure that this time she didn't escape.

"Yvonne, I love you, and I promise that we will get through this together and I will do everything in my..."

4

His last words were choked underneath a gulp of breathlessness as his eyes began to water.

After a while teary eyes turned into more sniffs and snuffles. Simon and Yvonne had been sat in Claire's bedroom for over an hour, Simon catching a glimpse of the time from Claire's *'every girl's **gotta** have one of these Mini Mouse clocks,'* realised that time was passing and they still needed to go and lay flowers where Claire's body was found. It was about a two and a half hour journey as it was, and they were running incredibly behind.

"I think it's time we got going, don't you think love?"
Yvonne looked up gazing into his eyes for about four seconds, and then nodded in agreement.

In the forest

She'd lost them. A whole big group of people had suddenly vanished before her eyes. Why? She did not know and how? She was certainly unsure. As she walked the dark ominous surroundings, she remained completely oblivious to the deserted destination in which she was. A look to her left, and up arose the black daunting vengeance of darkness, seizing her crystal green irises. A look to her right, it was as if ocular delusions of treacherous foul creatures blustered her brain. They gouged and snarled at her flesh as if it were some vivacious enterprise to eat. One look up and the gloomy appearance of the barbaric skies frowned down at her with grim-visage faces. A look down, she felt the grimy mounds of earth sinking deeply into the shattered soles of her petite feet. One look forward. Fear gripped her internal organs. Tension had captured her body, as if she

5

had been taken hostage. This was just the beginning. The beginning of Claire's mystery.

Voices. She heard voices. A whisper, whimpers, cries, laughs. Sounds. *Boom, Bang, Bang.* She heard sounds. People. Was it people she could hear?
***No!***
She felt like a mental patient, thinking she heard things that weren't even there.

"Hello, is anybody there… *anybody*?"
The awkwardness of silence taunted her. It made her feel exceedingly insignificant. It teased and tormented her. Mad. A series of various thoughts and emotions raced heavily, like flashes of burning lightning through her troubled mind. She solemnly longed, craved and hoped that she was not *alone.*

There was something very mysterious about this forest. She contemplated to herself on its sense of surrealism.

"*Claaiirrree…Claaiirre*" something anonymously whispered in the distance.

"*CLAIRE!*"
*What was that?* She turned in swift motion scanning her atmosphere with curiosity. Was she hearing things? Or did she really hear her name being called?

In the car

"It's strange innit? Very strange. I guess you don't expect your children to die before you." Yvonne still hadn't passed the stage of acceptance.

**10 minutes later…**

"Nearly there love," Simon turned to his wife, gracing her with his warm embrace. It was as if he hadn't even heard her speak a moment ago. He then glanced back to the site of the road, accepting the fact that he was probably going to be ignored.

"Umm hum," She responded randomly after a short period of time whilst blowing her frizzy hair back with a tremendous huff. She fidgeted impatiently in the car seat whilst continuously biting her nails until they were right down to the pink soft flesh on her fingers. Simon removed a hand from the steering wheel and pulled Yvonne's hands away from her mouth.

"Aren't you scared Simon?"

He looked at her briefly whilst trying to multi task his focus on the road at the same time.

"What made you ask that?"

"I don't know, well I guess maybe… because I am."

Leaving one hand on the wheel, he reached for her hand and placed it to his heart.

"Can you feel this beating?"

"Yes. *(Pause)* Yes I can, *very fast* actually."

"That's how scared I am."

Her hand remained there for a while before finally withdrawing it. Nothing more was said. I suppose there was nothing more to be said, and on they drove the rest of the journey in complete *silence.*

Back in the forest

Her throat stung for the yearning of a drink to quench her crusted ocsophagus. Reaching her hands nervously behind, fiddling for her rucksack, It was her great horror to find that it was no longer there. Vanished. Disappeared. Gone.

"My bag!"

At that, she panicked, becoming even more petrified. Her pace of walking became more active in motion.

"Somebody! Anybody?"

Claire wanted a way out; she was desperate and afraid. Speeding up even more, CRUNCH! Hesitating on her hands and knees she had stumbled. A crunchy familiar substance seemed to have disintegrated before her eyes. Staring at it, strangely, she picked it up examining its content carefully with great admiration.

"My, my bracelet?"

What on earth is it doing here? she wondered, and why was it so dirty and decrepit. Looking at it, she saw how its interior was slowly rotting away. *How strange! Wait a minute, what's going on?*

Suddenly, her eyes were drawn to another familiar object in the near distance. Getting back on her feet, she ran hastily over to where the object was visibly placed. She stopped herself immediately. On the ground was her rucksack, surrounded by red and white banners, *cordons*.

*Cordons, why are there cordons surrounding my rucksack?*

As she stood puzzled and extremely confused, she then began to notice more of her belongings scattered in the territorial area, and *flowers*.

*Flowers?*

*My face? Missing! What?*

*Claire! Dead?*

*Is this some kind of practical joke?* Claire became annoyed and frustrated at the sight of this.

*Why do they think I'm missing? Dead? I'm right here, lost, but fine, I don't understand!*

Tearing wildly through the banners, she grabbed hold of the newspaper article containing her face. In bold clear print it read…

**"Claire Robinson, aged 15, died 2 weeks ago after going on a school camping trip. It was claimed that she had wandered off; losing the rest of the group that she had come with. Unfortunately, after this incident she was not seen again, until her body was discovered shortly after, next to an endangered bush of thorns in the forest."**

Claire dropped the article to the ground instantly, her eyes widened and she started breathing heavily.

*WHAT huh! I huh, CAN'T huh, BE huh, DEAD huh!*

Her mind couldn't function properly and her breathing became even heavier. Tears began streaming down her pale face as she couldn't bring herself to believe the truth.

In the car

"You have arrived at your destination," the sat-nav announced boldly. Simon looked over to his nervous wreck of a wife, as she froze timidly on the car seat.

"It's time Yvonne."

"No, no, Simon, I can't do it, I really can't do this."
It was just too much, she was about to face the place where her only precious baby girl had lost her life.

"Yes you can," Simon reassured her, "we're in this together, are we not? I'm right here with you, don't be afraid." He managed to persuade her to get out of the car with a few words of comfort; he helped her along as her face hid away in his chest. She was like a lost puppy that had gone astray. Family and friends also followed them closely behind ready to say *goodbye*.

The forest was dead and dreary, Yvonne loathed the sight of it as she visualized her daughter lost, alone and afraid.

"My poor baby! My poor baby! She must have been so scared."

The thought of her being alone in such a forsaken environment was troubling to the mind.

Back in the forest

**Moments later…**

Claire watched as family and friends appeared before her very eyes.

"Mum! Dad!" she cried helplessly.

It was a relief to her soul to see them finally coming to her rescue. She felt loved once more as she could only assume that everybody had been looking for her all this time and now she was found.

They all began placing cards, more flowers and décor around the banners, whilst completely ignoring her presence. Claire found this rather strange. She then went closer to make sure that she could definitely be seen this time.

"Mum! Dad! Look it's me!" She reached out her arms; strangely, as she went to hug them she passed straight through them. She observed her arms and hands, *horrified* by what had just happened. So it was true, she was dead. Loud cries echoed through the atmosphere as people mourned deeply for her loss. Claire refused to give up easily; she couldn't quite come to terms with it all and refused to believe the truth.

**"NOOOO!! I'M NOT DEAD! LOOK, I'M HERE. MUM! DAD! NAN! ZOE! MAX! I'M HERE, LOOK, PLEASE**

**LISTEN TO ME! WHY ARE YOU INGNORING ME? PLEASE, I'M HERE!"**
Her loud cry for help, turned into a loud cry of tears for she had finally realised it was no use because they couldn't hear her.

I guess this was just another mystery. However, not just *any* mystery. *Claire's mystery.*

Twisted Tuesday

The sunrise shone brightly through the double-glazed windows as she lazed untidily in her bed. Her legs were spread widely, at the edges, as spit dribbled like a running tap from the sides of her thin lips. How *'unladylike,'* her mother always grunted, whilst doing her daily routine of attempting to drag her typical teen out of bed each morning.

"Time for school missy, UP, NOW!" she always yelled.
With her daughter's reply usually being just a "SNOOOOOOOOOOOOORE!" well that's if you can call *that* a reply. More like a hideous noise.

**An hour later…**
AAAAAAAAAAHHHHHHHHHHHHHHHHHHHHHHHH!!
The noise she usually made when she was late.

"What was I thinking? Too much TV last night, again."
She stumbled flat on her face landing in an awkward position on the bedroom floor with blue pillows and a cream duvet suffocating her entire face.

"I'M OK!" she shouted as if trying to reassure herself.
Glaring wide-eyed at her alarm clock, she had seen that it had gone off an hour ago. Rushing to her feet in a speedy flash with eye lids still half closed she threw herself into the long mirror hanging perfectly on the wardrobe door. "OMGOOOOSH!" she screamed to the horrendous look of the monster on the other side. She then dashed for the bathroom, having the quickest shower of her life. When finally dressed in the ugliest epic school uniform of educational history, she encountered the mirror once more.

"Right, only one way to fix this madness, COSMETICS!"
Number 1. Black mascara.
Number 2. Black Eyeliner.

Number 3. Foundation (which perfectly blended into her skin tone).

Number 4. A bit of blusher.

And finally Number 5. Just a touch of pink lip-gloss, (to finish the job).

"There, better already, Jasmine Kelly is ready to go." Plunging the skin beneath her eyes down, she tried to revamp the fat, lumpy white bags from under them. Finally, realising that she really had no more time for fanning around, she grabbed her funky-dory, and fresh 'Jane Norman' bag and headed down the stairs and out the front door.

Panting and puffing all over the place, she finally realised that wagging P.E lessons for the last year wasn't the wisest of choices. As she stopped to catch her breath, the school bus came speeding past.

"WAIIIIIIIIIIIIIIIIIIIIITTT!! NOO, STOP! STOP!" she yelled as she gasped for litres of oxygen. As she stopped running, she watched as the bus drove into the distance with familiar school faces staring, pointing and laughing out of the windows.

"ARRGGH! Just my luck, darn it!"

Time had passed and dragged on terribly. Jasmine refused to even bother to show her face on school grounds, instead she felt her day would be better spent wallowing in her own self-pity. I mean why should she care? It's not as if she wasn't just missing out on, I don't know, 6 whole hours of valuable education or something *silly* like that. If she had spent more time sleeping than watching the latest catch ups of 'Jeremy Kyle' on ITV1 then she wouldn't be in this mess now, would she? She huffed and puffed and blew a great steam of anger out.

Whilst walking down a deserted street of silent traffic and practically no atmosphere, a small ginger cat approached her.

"Get away you nuisance of a fur ball!" she shrieked, whilst looking at it with threatening body posture and wagging her fists in front of its face. Alarmed, the ginger cat ran off swiftly.

"Yeah, and good riddance to you too, I mean what do I look like, a vet?"

**10 minutes later….**
The ginger fluff ball had returned.

"For goodness sake, leave me alone will ya, I could have you done for stalking you know."
This time instead of running away, the ginger cat stayed put.

"Shoo! Go away! Grrrrhhh! Psssstt!!"
It still stood in refusal to budge; she folded her arms at his stubbornness to do as he was told.

"Fine then, be disobedient for all I care."
After a while she just possibly couldn't resist the velvet ginger fur and the black beady eyes, pure innocence, you could also call it.

"Ooh who am I kidding, I suppose you're cute, okay you can stay with me, I could do with the company anyway, just behave yourself erm… whatsyahface… Mr, that's it, I'll call you Mr!"
And on they both walked along the isolated pavement, side-by-side, hand in paw.

An irritating rattle hummed through Jasmine's ears, her view began to accelerate like a mammal with monocular vision. She couldn't quite distinguish where it was coming from. Suddenly looking down she saw Mr hitting an object with his paw. Its content looked exquisitely ravishing, but very delicate. It was layered in fine metallic gold décor, with the interior embroidered with sky blue jewels.

"Wow, it's absolutely gorge! Good boy Mr."
Jasmine ran behind a closed corner, Mr followed scurrying quickly behind. She didn't want anyone to see her new-found possession. She was highly fascinated as she shook it forcefully to see what it contained.

"AAAAAAAAAAAAAAHHHHH!" she shrieked.

"BOOM. BANG. BAAMM. CAABAZZ!" was the noise of the mighty explosion that had been unleashed from the golden object.

Jasmine couldn't believe the hazel pupil fragments of her eyeballs. Before her appeared an enormous blue creature, its black hair tied up high into a perfect ponytail, and its blue arms dressed in the shiniest gold bracelets she had ever seen.

"M, m, m, Mr! Mr," she screamed.
Glancing behind, Mr was nowhere to be seen.

"WHO DARES TO AWAKEN THE QUARTERS OF THE ALMIGHTY GENIE?!"

Jasmine, not knowing what to do or say for herself, stared straight back into the genie's eyes with nothing but confusion eating away at her mind. The genie gazed at her with a gruesome look of disgust with his black, menacing eyes.

"Little girl, are you deaf? Did you not hear my question? I demand you to answer me at once!" he bellowed.
Sweat showered Jasmine's forehead.

"My, my, my name...Erm... I have a name...erm it...it...it's J...Ja...Jas... Jasmine." Stuttering like a warm blooded mammal that had just been dropped into the base of Antarctica, she couldn't seem to make sense of any word, phrase or sentence that left her mouth.

"I'm afraid I don't speak the language of 'Gibberish', although my father did suggest for me to take it up at A-level, but never mind about that. Now, now where was I, Oh yes, I am growing sick and tired of amateurs like you, unleashing me from my, might I add, very comfortable lamp!"

Jasmine stood puzzled, having no idea what the genie was babbling on about.

"Now there, look, you see what I mean! The rudeness of you! Absolute cheek I tell you, if it were my way, I'd have your head! Now hurry up, make your three wishes, so I can pack up my books and tricks and be gone!" He folded his arms boldly while staring at Jasmine with one eyebrow raised towards the air.

"Now wait a minute Genie, well that's if you really are a genie, what on earth are you talking about? Wishes, tricks, what?"

A humungous purple vein emerged at the top of the genie's forehead.

"How dare you question if I'm a genie! Huh, am I a real genie? Of course I am a real genie, you dim-witted time waster of a human being! Now listen up good missy, cuz I'm only gonna say this once, and once only. Now here's the deal;

Number 1: Farse human unleashes Genie from lamp.

Number 2: Unfortunately Genie 'has' to grant farse human 3 wishes.

Number 3: Then farse human can get out of Genie's face and then Genie can, as they say, 'gwarn bout im business.' *CAPEESH!*"

The genie fumed so hard that steam was being released from his ears.

Jasmine pinched herself several times, just to make sure that she wasn't dreaming. Nope, turns out she was living in reality. Living it loud and clear! The genie grew impatient as he waited and waited for Jasmine. He dragged his thick blue eyelids down in front of his face with his broad blue fingertips, as if experiencing some form of mental break down.

Jasmine didn't know what to do. Whether to take this blue stranger seriously? Could he even be trusted? Did she have anything to lose by trusting him? She then sighed heavily, finally giving in and reassuring herself that she had nothing to lose.

"Right Genie, I've decided I have nothing to lose by attempting to trust you, I even take your every word even if it does sound a bit bizarre, besides I have nothing better to do and 3 wishes doesn't sound that bad I suppose, I could use a bit of fun to brighten this disastrous day anyway."

"Hmm, well then, I see you have finally smelt the hot chocolate and come to your senses, but just before you get all excited, I must inform you that with ALL, and I repeat with ALL 3 wishes you will receive a consequence."

"A consequence?" Jasmine questioned. "What do you mean a consequence? I'm sure Aladdin didn't have consequences with his wishes!"

"WELL MY DEAREST, I WOULD THEN ALSO LIKE TO POINT OUT THAT THIS ISN'T SOME POXY DISNEY MOVIE WITH CARTOON CHARACTERS, THIS IS 2000 AND BLOOMIN 9, SO GET WITH THE PROGRAMME EINSTEIN!"

Jasmine stood in a state of shock as the genie's every word echoed off the surface of her body, leaving her bewildered.

"Alright, alright, you don't have to shout you know, right wish number 1, hmmm let's see, think carefully Jas, think wisely," she murmured to herself. Rubbing the smooth contours of her chin, she wondered, thinking long and hard about what to ask for; she wanted something that would benefit the whole world and not just herself. But what could she ask for?

"It is 2072, and Jasmine is still thinking!" The genie muttered sarcastically. Finally, a huge grin spread across Jasmine's face.

"I know, I've got it, get ready for this one Genie, I wish for *'WORLD PEACE'.*"

**POOF!!** And it was done.

It was like rush hour on Boxing Day except people were rushing to greet one another. Jasmine's hand had been shaken by so many different strangers it grew tired and sweaty which actually made it feel quite repulsive.

"Whoa, talk about 'Living together in *perfect* harmony!'" She wasn't used to so much attention at one time, especially seeing as half the attention was from people she had never seen in her entire life. People wouldn't leave her alone, pulling, prodding and giving her huge bear hugs. It was almost as if she was being violated by people crossing over her personal space boundaries.

"That's enough!" she yelled as she stampeded through a crowd and headed for 'Curry's'. She found many electrical appliances to harbour behind, until she felt it was safe to leave. Facing ahead of her was a plasma, flat screen 30 inch TV.

"Wow!" Jasmine gasped in amazement. "I bet Jeremy Kyle would look even better on that." She drew closer to it sneakily, trying not to blow her cover; Gordon Brown was on there, giving another speech in the Houses of Parliament.

"Aye? What's this?" Jasmine had to check if her ears were deceiving her. "WHAT? NOO! They are not serious! They can't do this!"

The biggest most absurd crisis had occurred, and by the looks of things there was nothing Jasmine could do. The EU had agreed on sending all children in Europe to school 7 days a week. There were even interviews shown with parents and children agreeing to this decision. Everyone was agreeing with one another, even if decisions were as ridiculous as this one.
Jasmine had quite frankly had enough, and didn't even hesitate to un-wish such a deranged nightmare before things really did get out of hand.

"And 5, 4, 3, 2, 1…BINGO! Oh back so soon Jas," the genie laughed hysterically with his bulging stomach flubbing up and down like a trampoline.

"That wasn't funny Genie," She hissed, pulling an evil look out of the corner of her eye. "And by the way it's Jasmine to you."

"Hey, hey, hey, I did warn you, so don't get all 'MISS DIVA FEISTY FABULOUS' with me honey," He waved and clicked his hands in the air imitating someone with a diva-ish manner.

Anyhow, swiftly moving on, time for your second wish, or do you need some recovery time from that dreadful last wish, hmm??" The genie was purposely winding Jasmine up, and she knew it.

"NO, I don't need 'recovery time,' thank you. I am quite ready to make my second wish," she smiled at him smugly trying not to be discouraged by his mocking.

Thinking long, hard and more carefully about what she was going to ask for this time, she had decided on a second wish.

"SHUT MY MOUTH AND CALL ME BRUCE WILLIS, I'VE GOT IT! ... *'I WISH TO BE THE RICHEST PERSON IN THE WORLD!'*"

**POOF!** And it was done.

Masses of money stacked in numerous piles surrounded her environment as she sat prestigiously on her royal throne.

"Yes Miss Kelly."

"Right away Miss Kelly."

"As you wish Miss Kelly." Servants and butlers acted within an instant on her every wish and command. It was all just too much. Just too much for her to believe. Diamonds, rubies and pearls were visible on every body part known to the human-race.

"OMG! OMG! I have golden eyelashes! I have golden eyelashes! This is Crazy!" Yes, 'tis true, she had the whole enchilada and much more.

Her fingers had grown tired from all the clicking and snapping she had been doing for the last hour. To her advantage, she had been provided with a special cream from one of her butlers to relieve these aches in her fingertips. Unbelievable, there was actually something for everything in her kingdom.

"I want!"

"I want!"

"I want!"

It just kept coming up, like word vomit. She wasn't about to let this once in a lifetime experience pass her by lightly, she was taking advantage of every opportunity she was given.

As she soaked up the tremendous new life-style that she was now living and breathing, an alarm sounded with a loud triumph. The atmosphere was no longer filled with glistening spot lights of antique chandeliers, but with red flashing warning lights along with the daunting repetition of the word 'INTRUDERS!'

The entire kingdom rushed around beneath her feet frantically.

"RING THE ALARM!"

"BOLT THE DOORS!"

"RUN FOR YOUR LIVES!"

"EVERY MAN FOR THEMSELVES!"

Anxious to know what on earth was going on, Jasmine Kelly demanded an explanation and she wanted one urgently.

"You there!" she hurled pointing her index finger directly towards a lost looking servant trying to find an escape route.

"Y-ye-yes your highness," he stuttered nervously as his hands hid deep inside his mouth.

"I demand you to give me an explanation for this chaos, FILTH, disruption to my kingdom!"

"The kingdom is under attack your majesty!"

Her eyebrow rose sharply towards the air, she grew impatient at this grumbling fool before her eyes stating the very obvious.

Sarcastically she replied, "You don't say," as if she didn't hear the irritating and loud repetition of 'INTRUDER!' like everybody else. She continued, "My question is WHY?"

The servant began laughing hysterically.

"Something funny?!" she was not in the least amused.

"Your highness, your kingdom is under attack at approximately every 7 hours without fail. You're the

22

richest person in the world, and everybody wants your money."

She sat back a moment, realising what she had bargained for. Genie did say my every wish had a consequence, she remembered.

"Will my life be like this forever servant....servant? Servant?" Looking around, the servant was no longer in her sight. It really was every man for themselves. She knew her life wasn't safe to live like this, and she didn't want to live it in fear for the rest of her days.

"No! Enough! Enough! I shall not live my life in fear! No more! GENIE MAKE IT ALL STOP!"

"Oh back so soon," the genie laughed whilst manicuring his nails.

"It's not funny!"

The genie sarcastically held up his thumbs and index fingers on both hands displaying the letter 'W'.

"And what's that supposed to mean?"

My gosh, this child is stupider than I thought.

"It means, Jasmine, 'WHATEVER!'"

She tutted and puffed at the genie's immaturity.

"I have no time for your shenanigans Genie!"

Holding up the 'W' sign again, he began to remind her that she only had one more wish left.

5, or maybe even 10 minutes had passed on by now…

Another 5 minutes….

Another, perhaps 20…

"20 BLOOMIN 99!"

"Alright! Alright! I'm sure genies aren't supposed to hassle the person doing the wishing."

"I don't really care what you think, I'm not any ordinary genie, I'm a unique individual and never to be compared, FURTHERMORE! I would suggest that you think wisely about this LAST AND FINAL (Praise the Lord!!!!) wish."

23

Completely blocking out the genies negative energy, Jasmine tried long and hard to find herself in deep, serious thought for her **last, final** wish…………………………………………………………………...

…………………………………………………………………………

…………………………………………………………………………

…………………………………………………………………………

…………………………………………………………………………

…………………………………………………………………………

…………………………………………………………………………

## …FINALLY!!

She had thought of a 3$^{rd}$ wish.

"I've got it! I've got it!" she exclaimed excitedly, whilst jumping up and down through the mid air like an eager bird ready to take flight. The genie almost had a panic attack, as Jasmine had woken him out of his midday nap.

"Goodness, what year are we in now?"

Putting her hands on her hips, she shook her head at his sarcasm.

"Ha-ha! Very funny, but seriously, listen up carefully, cuz this is a good one. I wish for '*CONTINUOUS GOOD HEALTH.*'"

**POOF!** And it was done. Just like that.

She was fit. She was healthy. She was more than well. She felt ALIVE! She was beautiful. ☺

It was 6:00am on a hot summer's morning and Jasmine had just been for her 2-hour morning jog. Feeling refreshed she sat on the front step of her small bungalow, enjoying the sunrays that graced her cheekbones invitingly. She had never felt this way before, it was better than peace, it was better than riches. It was the BEST she had felt in all her life.

Her face had suddenly frozen in deep horror as an ugly frail lady walked by on her path. Her skin was saggy and carelessly hung from her body; it was an awful sight. Her eyes blood shot from what looked like endless nights of constant tears. Jasmine couldn't help but wonder what was wrong; she followed the lady. As she finally caught her up, she snatched her hand back firmly.

"Excuse me, I know this may seem so rude, and I know you don't know me, however I couldn't help but notice, that you looked so sad."
The lady couldn't even look into Jasmine's face properly as if she were ashamed of her own appearance. She then began sobbing uncontrollably, tear after tear.

"Oh, if you only knew child! If you only knew! Do you even know who I am? An athlete, a great athlete. One of the best I was, one of the very best. You wouldn't believe it though I mean look at me now, just look at me. I was so fit, so healthy, so beautiful; it was literally as if someone had sucked the life out of me. Now look at me, no one has an answer to why this has suddenly happened. No one has the answer. It's so sad; the doctor said that there is not much hope left for me now."

The old lady struggled free from Jasmine's grip, continuing on the path alone and completely miserable. Jasmine covered her mouth with her hand, as if trying to restrain herself from revealing the truth to the poor, innocent frail lady.

"Oh no! What have I done? This is all my fault."
Jasmine couldn't bear to face what she had caused; she had no intention of harming anybody else's health when she wished this wish. There was only one way she could fix such a disaster and she knew how.

Back to reality. No more wishes. It was a relief to Jasmine's traumatised mind. She contemplated on what she had experienced and what a great pleasure it was to be back to normal living all over again. She could have been forced to go to school seven days a week, subjected to money-hungry intruders every 7 hours for the rest of her life or she could have destroyed the innocent life of another human being.

What a tragedy, she thought. Once again, she stood in deep thought awhile, of course not for too long with the helpful interruption of the genie.

"Well, that was fun wasn't it!" the genie chuckled whilst displaying a huge line of gleaming white teeth and high cheekbones. Jasmine looked straight back into the genie's face, and instead of retaliating to his irritating sarcasm, she simply graced him with a lovely and genuine smile.

"You know what Genie; I would like to thank you. Before meeting you I really thought my life was full of bad luck and downfalls. But after experiencing what I have experienced today, it's just made me come to the realisation that really I haven't got it that bad after all."

The genie floated puzzled and confused. Usually at the end of 3 wishes he expected his candidates to be miserable, but not Jasmine. He began to wonder where exactly he went wrong and if he had done his job properly this time round.

"I'm afraid I don't quite understand," he finally responded after a brief period of time of thinking to himself.

"I'm saying that 'Bad Luck' doesn't exist."

"OH!" he paused, not quite understanding Jasmine's conclusion either.

"Oh Genie! Never mind," she laughed.

Shaking his hand grippingly, she thought that she would at least attempt the last 2 periods of what was left of school.

"Where are you going?" the genie questioned.

"To make the most of my life!" she shouted back as she hurried along the path.

The genie glared wide-eyed as if he were in some immortal shock at Jasmine's positive attitude towards the outcome of the situation at hand. He watched her slim, tall figure with great interrogation but not with the slightest of amusement. Sticking his tongue out after her he finally dismissed the situation holding up the 'W' sign once more.

"YOU THINK YOUR ALL THAT, BUT YOUR NOT, JASMINE KELLY!" he bellowed aggressively after her.

"Bye Genie, don't feel discouraged, have a good life, seriously." And off she went into the distance going to make the most of life, just like she said.

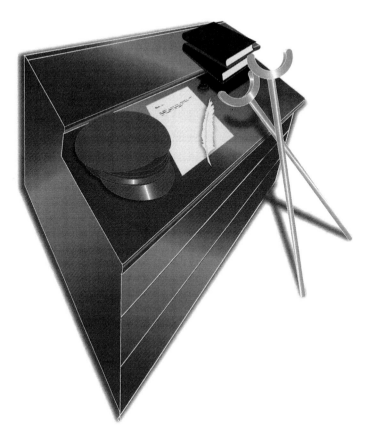

# The Feeling of War....

<u>September 1919</u>

Dear Diary,
        The feeling of war. I remember it like the days of yesteryears. How do I even begin to describe such an intense experience or even journey? The endless days, the eerie nights.

"FLASHBACK!"

Wait. This may take a moment.

    Andre Hope is my name. Hope. Quite a powerful last name. Hope. It was hope that made me exceedingly determined to survive the oppressive, burdensome feeling of war. It was a hope that gave me the strength, the courage and the faith to face the scornful gaze of *fear*. So, what is hope? A feeling of desire. A possibility of fulfilment. Those are just two definitions of the word. However, I define it as the key. The key to unlock the door of the future. My future.

Look and read carefully.
**This is my story. . . .**

## August 1914 – The Battle of the Somme

Dear Diary,

The ships progressed closer and closer towards the dominating hedgehogs that attempted to stop us from entering the restricted territories of the German forces. I watched in aberration as soldiers continuously vomited, some with consistently shaking hands, some with hands clasped together or holding their sacred crosses and praying deeply for the sake of their own lives.

Boom! Crash! Bang! The atmosphere changed, immediately contrasting dramatically to what it was 5 minutes before. It was loud and aggressive. A series of gas bombs and bullets sharply flew in my immediate direction. Soldiers panicked, moving swiftly up and down the ship. Many went overboard in an attempt to save themselves. They were so scared they forgot that they were carrying heavy luggage, ironically contributing to their own deaths as one by one they drowned. Our army was vulnerable in comparison to the powerful force of our allies. For a split moment, the atmosphere muffled around me, I was unable to hear anything. Trudging through the glacial blood filled waters; I was diverted constantly as masses of dead bodies interfered in my path. An explosion alerted my hearing once more. Searching anxiously for cover, without hesitating I ran at a rapid pace.

Knowing I couldn't stop, knowing that death was strong enough to overtake me, knowing that I wanted to survive, I knew anything was possible at this moment in time. Thinking of where I was going didn't actually once occur to me, strangely. I just had to get out of sight and soon. Stumbling here and there over several dead bodies delayed even more of my precious time, and encouraged more of my frustration.

Oh no! What was happening? The irritable feeling of fear struck my stomach as I watched a group of threatening figures move towards me swiftly. They were all securely armed. I clearly had no chance of survival, I thought hope had failed me; I was completely defenceless against them. A great beautiful blaze of bright lights filtered through the air as they began to shoot wildly with their guns. Having no occasion to appreciate this scenery, I stopped, dropped and rolled, stretching my body to its full extent; long and tall across the ground. I was hoping to be camouflaged between whatever rubble was surrounding me. Sweat rained on me like a running waterfall as I waited in the anxious silence. I could no longer hear a sound, maybe it was a trap. Should I take the risk? No! Yes? I couldn't hear a sound, what was I to do? I couldn't take this anxious feeling of waiting any longer as the intrusive silence provoked me abundantly like the irritating presence of a fly flitting around. The creak of daylight echoed against the clouds as I sat and gazed helplessly, as if crying out to the merciless skies. The impatience of my nature had grown into a sluggish manner of complete rage.

Then began the clamorous noise of the death prone targets once more. Shutting the battered, black eyelids upon my scarred face, I began to pray solemnly. The never ending sounds increased the running pulse of my heartbeat to a rapid pace that ventured into the near motion of bursting out the delicate flesh of my agonizing chest.

With an immediate haste, the boisterous commotion died abruptly into the distance. The shots had finally drawn to a close. They had stopped. Gone. Vanished. Elapsed completely, at such random timing. After a substantial amount of time, thinking that the coast was now clear, I steadily got back onto my feet. I began to make my way in an attempt to reunite myself back with the rest of my troop. As I made gradual steps, my movement was cut short, as something was not right. A familiar uninviting noise made me eminently uncomfortable. As I went to resume my original shelter of cover, it was then too late. Oh no! I was wrong. I was DOOMED! In a split instant, I was suddenly greeted with the tremendous presence of a pollutant fumed gas bomb. Losing all sense of gravitational force it flew me violently in the daunting atmosphere of mid-air; landing with my spine harshly against the huge, hardened surface of a grey crinkled rock.

# Was this the end?

<u>**A week later August 1914**</u>

Dear Diary,

Is it over? Please tell me it is. Maybe it is. Could it be? Maybe, I'm about to be awakened from this disastrous nightmare, to be surrounded by the faces of those dearest to my heart. My dear Papa and Mama, my angelic wife and three beautiful children. I was clearly attempting to delude myself. This is the tragedy of reality, and here I was living it. Living it loud and clear!

I've been sitting here in the chancy war battlefield for what seems like forever in the unaccompanied presence of myself. Tediously waiting. Just a lonely soldier, in obsolete conditions, after a horrific, barbarous bloody war.

A tidal wave of various emotions and feelings has captured the depths of my confounded brain. Placing them underneath a heinous sluggish tide of doom. I've lost all sense of pride, my dignity and respect. I feel the great devastation of exposure and humility. I felt absolutely helpless at this present moment in time. I have clearly been abandoned. Deserted. Left behind. Left to face the grim-visage, belligerent faces of my adversaries. Adversaries who despise me and my country. Adversaries who are able to take away the precious being of a life and re-claim it as their vivacious victory!

I feel incredibly, unbearably, alone. The gross feeling of mucilaginous mud sinks deeply through my shattered clothing onto my tender anus, making my body wince in disgust. The hard encased material of my helmet submerges my forehead forcefully trying to blind my vision, as I sit miserably in doubt with my elbows on the hinges of my tiresome knee caps. Yes, you could say I am in complete and utter despair. I didn't think it was possible for any one to understand how I was feeling. Nobody knew the trouble I had foreseen. Nobody knew the sorrow that had overcome my joy.

The remains of disaster encompassed the entire atmosphere. Battered machinery, guns, army wear. They all lay clearly in my distanced scenery. Giving me no sense of hope. Not even dead bodies were here to grace me with their presence, as well as comfort. I refused to look back to the tragic memories of the past week. I refused to look to my left nor right, or even up to the intimidating polluted clouds, as their grey bodies frowned down fiercely onto the Earth. I only chose to look ahead, seeing nothing. Nothing.

Nothing, but the horrendous fate of delusions and the elongated days of darkness ahead of me.

**SILENCE!** Not a peep. Nor a sound. All was quiet. Too quiet. The constant revisitation of howling winds pimpled my shivering skin like symptoms of severe acne. The sound continuously grew louder and louder, penetrating itself at lightning pace through the ringing dark tombs of my ear drums. It suddenly **stopped**! I then began to reminisce about the raging cries. Screams and sounds of agony I once heard. It was all just like a hideous nightmare. Tears wet the sides of my swollen cheeks as I began to realise the blessing bestowed upon my life, as I was still alive and waiting. Waiting to be rescued. I contemplated on how the atmosphere had incredibly revamped its form into the golden sound of complete muteness!

The swine intoxication of doom entered through the air holes of my stiffened still nose. The stinky stench of fresh, red blood, entwined itself vastly into the formidable open atmosphere of the deeply blackened skies. The clouds looked extremely heavy in weight as they hung dramatically into the territory of Earth. They unleashed the revolting smell of toxic gases that severely stung my innocent eyes; making them shed uncontrollable anguishing tears of fear and desperation. I coughed repeatedly like in the midst of a harrowing spasm as more fumes began to accelerate through my body piercing my insides, and clinging resolutely to the back of my throat.

Groping the ground with firm intensity, I felt the mounds of artificial banks and earth slice against fragments of my swollen wrists; leaving them in more agonizing pain. I started sweating heavily, as if being chased by a vicious mob of fierce warriors. Biting my once smooth, now crusted lips, I tried with all my might to enclose the unbearable feeling of all the excruciating pain.

# 10 minutes
# And
# 4 seconds later…

My shins were numb and faulty as I could barely move them. This atrocious experience had become more than overwhelming. It was overbearing. Finally, removing my hands from the dead ground, I clasped them harshly over my face. I wished for my grungy nail beds to render the weak flesh from my cheeks. However, being wise I sat in refusal to cause anymore brutal affliction to my already damaged temple.

# Still waiting ….

Time passes.
Time had passed.

Time was still passing.
I was still waiting.
I am still alive.
Why? Why had no one come to rescue me yet? Was I so unimportant, so unremembered that people didn't even so much as notice my existence. It was all just too much. I was angry! FURIOUS! Tired of waiting. The thought that I might die a lonely soldier, in unfamiliar surroundings, without having a chance to see my family again was too much to even take into account.

## A moment of Hope...

A sharp noise entered my ears. My body was too stiff to encourage any movement in my neck to look around. I easily distinguished what the sound was as it drew closer towards me. Before my eyes, I saw a truck arriving to where I had been situated miserably for days on end. **I was being rescued.** Finally. At last. Can you believe it? Someone had come to rescue me. Someone cared enough to ensure my survival. For the first time in my life, I felt worthy. My life did have worth. I realised that I had the **right** to live just as much as any other soldier who precariously risked their life for their country. That's when I believed. I believed with all my might that 'hope' couldn't have failed me yet. It would never fail me.
**Andre Hope.**

<u>September 1919</u>

Dear Diary,

This experience had brought me to the realisation of reality. It dawned on me, that wherever there is death, there can still be life. My life. Although war had extracted my legs, it still didn't take away the valuable qualities that define who I am. It didn't take my dignity, it couldn't take my pride. And most of all it didn't take me. I am a noble, brave young man. What I had achieved for my country is to be greatly admired and a highlighted memory for as long as I shall live.

So, what was my deepest fear? Inadequacy? I am powerful beyond all measure. I am who I am, not just because of the things I say, but what I have experienced. That is why I am here to say…

You have feelings,

I have feelings.

*However, only some can describe the true feeling.*

## *The feeling of war.*

Snow Black & The Seven Rastas

Far far away in the hot, exotic island of Jamaica, behind the tall palm trees, beyond the white-sandy beaches and tropical waters lived a beautiful, ravishing princess known as Snow Black. Oh and what a radiant sight she was, her skin was a smooth, dark glowing brown, like thick, creamy, rich Cadbury's chocolate. Her hair short and soft, combed perfectly into a fluffy, light afro, decorated with a yellow rose at the side; her thick lips sparkled permanently from the sweet strawberry gloss they were coated in and her broad chocolate buttoned nose sat promptly fixed in perfect proportion with the rest of her face. She was a Coca Cola bottle figure, emphasising her thick, well rounded curves. Natural born beauty they said, neither spot nor blemish, no cosmetics, just a natural, born beauty.

Unfortunately, her mother died when she was only a youngling, leaving her to fend for herself against her evil step-father. He was scornful and despised Snow Black. He mistreated her severely day by day; locking her away in the dark, deserted, unknown depths of the black dungeon, feeding her tiny crumbs of stale hardoe bread and a few sips of coconut water. Oh, how she pleaded for his mercy, oh how she wanted to flee and never return.

Many years had passed on by this time, and Snow Black had grown even more, into one of the most elegant, desirable ladies ever seen. As she rose from her bedside gracefully each morning, she was greeted with the joyful tune of birds singing in sweet unison. Nature adored her very presence, her sweet smelling scent and gleaming smile warmed their hearts. She was banished from the sight of her evil step-father, so she spent her days writing creatively in her trusted journal or sitting on the wide ledge of her window, staring yearningly out towards the rich blue skies, watching the white furry cushions as they sat within it, slowing passing by. She only hoped and prayed every single second that something or someone would come to her rescue, and sweep her out of sight, as far away from her evil step-father as she could get, away into a land filled with happiness.

"Mirror! Mirror! Pon de wall a whu da most gud looking nest of dem all?"
This was the repetitive phrase that the evil step-father never ceased to boom at the colossal mirror hanging lamentably on the wall each day. The mirror would then reply by saying, "Bwoi sah yu luk good, but Snow Black luk betta dan yu man!"
"Back foot! Yu lie! Yu lie! A wah yu say, yu a tek bad tings mek joke!"
"No man a nuh lie mi a tell, a true, a true!"
The evil step-father would burn with fury and envy at Snow Black's beauty when he heard this response. His patience could no longer be tested any further; he had had enough. It was not long after that he requested that Snow Black be killed.
When Snow Black heard such horrific news, she was overwhelmed tremendously with fear and anxiety. It was then that she built up the determination that she must escape. Her evil step-father's actions had left her no choice. She didn't want to die, and refused to give him the satisfaction. She ran and ran far far away into the deep, shadowy depths of the territorial Yam-Yam forest. She ran for hours, as far as her stylish gladiator sandals could carry her. She carried on running, maybe a day or two but she refused to stop, not until she was certain that she was safe and not until she knew she was as far away as possible.

Now during this particular moment in Jamaica the weather had brought the most unexpected gift. Snow? Yes snow indeed. Snow Black adored the very essence, as she loved the presence of snow. The trees shared their white coats openly as they bowed forthwith as if inviting Snow Black into their palm leaves for warmth. The ground carried her feet carefully as they soaked her footprints in remembrance. It was a gift especially for her.

Eventually, after such a tiresome and seemingly never ending journey she discovered an extravagant, elaborate mansion. The silver gates shone radiantly in the sharp horizon. The scorching yellow substance lying succulently waiting, in a blue embedded duvet of white cushions, reflected its surface, whilst slowly causing the snow to disappear. These were the superior gates that held the elegant entrance to what beheld prestigious courts. Something new. Something different. Something unique. The mansion was coated in a metallic gold paint as it towered high, standing so tall and wide as if defining that this territory only belonged to itself. And it alone. It was surrounded with a humongous banquet of luscious plantation such as yellow daffodils, purple hyacinths, blue tulips, pink carnations, white lilies, red roses and numerous rows of ital herbs. They were all planted perfectly in columned rows standing graciously upright in position. Snow Black questioned, to herself, how it was even possible for them to survive due to the conditions they were in. They stood along the hedges of the green marbled pathway, detailed with the fine intricate décor of crystallised sequences of multi-coloured gems that sparkled like glowing stars. The path was long and regal like the entry to the red carpet, but without the extreme bright flashes of white lights.

When the seemingly never ending path had drawn to a

close, before it stood a huge door. The door to the inside was beautifully two toned with shades of brown; ecru a greyish-pale yellow and russet, a brown colour with a reddish tinge. It had two large golden handles on the left and right along with a matching gold bell that played a sweet harmonious tune when rung.

Beyond the doors lay the foundation of luxurious quarters. Vibrant colours lit the atmosphere from the ceiling to the polished tiled floors, which reflected the image of every object in its view with perfect accuracy. The atmosphere was alive, warm and inviting. The walls were covered in mustard yellow that smiled brightly. Moving on further began the entrance to the tranquil living area. Its sense of peace and purity was enough to refresh the state of a stressful mind; everything that it contained sat in a gentle nature. There were white fluffy sofas that were so deep that an infant's body would be able to sink into its stomach comfortably. White cushions of all different shapes and sizes filled the sofas; some were also laid neatly around the edges of the room.

To the left of this room was an opulent dining area, It contained a long glass table which looked delicate enough to break with the tap of a finger nail. Above it was a majestic silver chandelier that hung in dignity, high and proud. The table was laid with clear wine glasses and the lustrous sheen of sterling silver cutlery laid in precise order.

"Coo yah de place luk gud!" she exclaimed breathlessly. She had never seen such a wonderful sight in all her days. Without further ado or hesitant reaction she wanted to see more. A complete stranger, completely oblivious to where she was, she stood in amazement at her surroundings. Searching the site of the complex house, she had no intention of leaving without seeing all the rooms or at least gracing them with her presence. Excitement bloomed throughout her like a bunch of flower buds opening in the season of spring. It was a memorable moment, maybe the best moment in her life so far.

"A wah dis?" she questioned while picking up an old Bob Marley record she found lying between a large case of other various records.

"Buffalo Soldier! Woi, dis a mi jam man!"
She immediately placed the record onto a glamorous, silver, record player that she had seen in the corner of the room. Snow Black danced and danced around for hours on end, doing tasteless, vulgar actions such as the Butterfly, the Bogle, Shelly Belly and even the Dutty Wine. Was this even legal you may ask? Of course it was, just harmless fun in the eyes of Snow Black, who at this point in time couldn't have given a single care in the world whether it was legal or not.

Meanwhile back at the palace, Snow Black's evil step-father was absolutely furious that she had escaped so quickly and easily, even after all the traps he had set to make sure that this was impossible. He knew that she had grown too smart for him now, he tried to devise a plan to be rid of her once and for all, but until one came to mind, for the time being, he would send out a search party of seven hundred soldiers to find her.

"FINE ER! FINE ER," he ordered.


"MI NUH BUSINESS IF SHE DEAD OR ALIVE! AN NUH BADDA CUM BACK WIDOUT HER!"

Back at the luxurious mansion, Snow Black had become overly exhausted after releasing some serious energy from dancing for so long. Ready for a rest, she ran up the delicate steps of the grand glass staircase, to find a choice of seven large bedroom suites appear before her very eyes. Which one to choose? It was such a difficult decision, all of them were so beautiful, minus the fact that they all contained ash-trays. However, she had finally brought herself to choose one. The suite she had chosen was all white, from the ceiling, to the carpet, even the furniture and the quilt covers! It was such a tranquil environment to be in, she fell in love with the feeling it gave to her. Before shutting her eyes to partake in a brief beauty rest, she couldn't help but wonder to herself, "Whu wudda need seven large bedroom suites?" Yawning with a triumphant noise, she fell fast into a deep peaceful sleep.

Many seconds turned into minutes which then turned into hours. By now, Snow Black was in a deep, peaceful sleep. For such a beautiful princess, her sleeping manners were not as graceful. She was completely ignorant as to what was going on around her. By now, it hadn't even occurred to her that she had been trespassing in the home of seven Rastas until ….

"A WHU DIS IN MI BLARSTED BED TU BACKSIDE?!"

With that, the rest of them came rushing in.

"Kekeh, what a feisty pickney eeh, yuh shud trow are out a door!"

Suddenly, in the blink of an eye awoke Snow Black to face the astonished facial expressions of seven complete strangers all staring directly at her.

"Aah! Get out mi face nuh!" howled Snow Black.

"Backfoot! A dupey! A dupey!"

She jumped straight out the bed within an instant, holding a pillow that partially covered her startled face as some sort of defence. She didn't know what to do with herself.

"Whey mi deh? A who yuh?" she questioned.

"Chu nah gyal, yuh nearly mek me have a heart attack, yuh in wei yard to backfoot, we shud be askin you de same ting."

With a quick interruption the other Rastas, were so mesmerised at Snow Black's unique beauty they zoomed past to get a good and closer look at her.

"Ooh gyal yuh luk gud man!"

"Yeh man, yuh luk fresh!"

"Real nice!"

"Mek me luk pan yuh face…WOII!"

"Whu yuh? Whu yuh? Whu yuh?" Snow Black asked and asked once again. The attention became flustering.

Suddenly, one of the Rastas began to beat box, then joined in another with humming, then another with patting a rhythmic tune on his knee, then another with clicking. Then began the singing.

"Well mi name is one, Ziggy, an mi love fi jiggy. Dis a two, Reggae. Three, Rum. Four, Pumpkin. An dat a five, Dumplin im Chickin is finga lickin. Den yuh hav six, Tom-Tom. An las but no least yuh hav seven, Big-bwoi an im caan eats sah!"

After introducing themselves in such an unusual choice of song, it was then that Snow Black started to feel more at ease.

"An wha shud we call yuh mi darlin'?"

"Snow Black, mi name is Snow Black."

"Snow Black, wat a pretty name eeh!" Ziggy exclaimed.

"An wat bought yuh so far into de deep, depths of Yam Yam Forest?"

"Mi so so sorry, but mi caan explain for intruding in all yuh yard. Mi hav waan wicked step-father yuh sei, an im wan fi kill mi, so mi add to escape."

"Coo yah im wan fi kill yuh, im wicked man!"

"Mi knuw, dats why mi ere."

The seven Rastas were very sympathetic towards Snow Black's situation, although she was a complete stranger and realistically a trespasser.

Meanwhile, back at the palace, the evil-step father had eventually been notified of where Snow Black currently was. Killing her the way he first intended would be much too easy, so he devised an even better plan of how to be rid of her once and for all. This time, his scheming idea was cunning and sneaky; he decided to send out one of his royal assistants disguised as a sweet elderly lady. He then gave the royal assistant a bottle of poisoned ginger beer to give to Snow Black. The bottle was wrapped decoratively with pink and yellow ribbon and a humongous silver bow just to top it off tastefully. His only wish was to outsmart Snow Black one day and he actually believed that this was going to work.

However, back at the luxurious mansion, the seven Rastas had made Snow Black feel at home. They welcomed her wholeheartedly into their home to stay as long as she needed to. To celebrate her arrival they had cooked up a big, scrumptious banquet of Caribbean dishes. There was ackee and saltfish, curry goat, jerk chicken, barbeque chicken, lobster, crab, rice and peas, fried dumpling, plantain, sweet potato, yam, pumpkin, hardoe bread, patties, festival, macaroni cheese, fry fish and run-dung, blue draaws, cow cock soup, stew peas and much, much more. It was a mighty, wondrous and delicious feast, never to be forgotten. Snow Black ate so fast that she drew the immediate attention of the seven Rastas as they watched her literally clean the whole table. To their amazement they would have never have thought her appetite would be so big with her having such a slim-lined figure. She had eaten so much her belly became overly bloated, causing a button to pop off her dress.

"Woi sah! Yu sure can cook Dumpling, tank yuh ever so much," she said in a very appreciative manner.

"Tank yu mi darlin', anytime, anytime," he smiled in response.

After a game of limbo and musical statues, the seven Rastas had to leave awhile to plant crops and some more ital herbs in their fields. They left Snow Black sitting cosily by the fire in a rather large mustard coloured rocking chair. She sat happily whilst humming joyful tunes to herself. She had never felt so happy in all her life; it was the experience of freedom.

Her ears were then alerted, as there was a loud knock on the door. She assumed it would be Big-bwoi coming back for more food. She opened the door, not knowing the precarious situation she was about to enter into. To her surprise, a sweet looking elderly lady stood before her eyes. She was very petite and looked fragile; she wore a navy blue frock patterned in tropical flowers, along with eccentric pearl earrings, necklace and bracelet.

"Hello mi darlin'," greeted the elderly lady.

"Hello mam, wah caan a duh fi yuh?"

"Well mi was jus passin' through de forest and mi cum across dis beautiful mansion dat did stand out from afar, so mi taught mi shud bring sum ginger beer cum as a gift for de person who own it."

"Oh how kind of yuh mam, tank yuh very much an God' Bless." Snow Black smiled gently at the sweet elderly lady's generosity while retrieving the poisonous bottle right from her very hands.

"You're welcome mi darlin', an mi shud be off now, take care."

"Ok, bye mam."

Snow Black couldn't help but admire the lovely decorating on the bottle; she also couldn't help but admire the fact that the elderly lady had been so kind. However, Snow Black did find it a bit strange that an elderly lady was wandering around and about in the deep, territorial depths of Yam-Yam Forest by herself. Oh well, that wasn't the point was it, the point was there was still some good left in the world and if the elderly lady wanted to be so generous then who was Snow Black to question this. She poured the contents carefully into a large glass making sure that she didn't spill a drop, she wasn't about to let any of this ginger beer go to waste. Gulping it down quickly, she loved the lingering sweet taste it left on the tip of her tongue. She had a craving; she poured another glass, then another, and then impatiently she just drank the rest from the bottle itself.

"Woi sah dat was nice man!"

THUD! In an instant, Snow Black fell to the ground. No, she was not dead like the evil step-father had intended, however she was unconscious from the poisoned drink.

Moments later, the seven Rastas had returned from the fields and were horrified to see Snow Black lying stiffly sprawled out on the living room floor.

"Oh Lard God! A wah happen to she," panicked Pumpkin as he walked round in circles on himself.

"Snow Black! Snow Black! Wake up nuh man! A wah wrong wid yuh?" cried Ziggy.

"Snow Black, yuh dead?" shouted Reggae.

"NOOO!!!" bawled Dumplin.

The seven Rastas did everything in their power to try and wake up the damsel in distress. They tried to resuscitate her, they tried playing loud music they even threw the remains of mutton gravy on her face. It was no

49

use; there was not a single word, action nor response from Snow Black. They had to accept the situation that was at hand once and for all. The fact of the matter was Snow Black was dead and there was nothing they could do about it. Whether they had chosen to accept this was a different matter altogether.

After moments of awkward silence …

"Well sah, we cyaan jus leave her deh suh jus sprawl out sprawl out pon de floor like dis," said Tom–Tom, whilst dabbing the mutton gravy off Snow Black's face with a damp paper towel.

"I'm right man, we hav to bury are," suggested Big-bwoi while munching quickly on a piece of tasty jerk chicken leg.

Within three days, the seven Rastas had built Snow Black a glass coffin. Their blood, sweat and tears went into it literally. It sparkled lustrously in the bright morning sunshine. They placed in it primroses and daises, then carefully Snow Black's tender body was placed in the centre of it. They carried her to the fields where they had prepared the funeral ceremony. Dumplin nearly dropped the coffin on the way as he was mourning for the loss of Snow Black. He was not alone in this, as it was too much for all of them to bear. It was so strange as they were mourning for a person they barely even knew, but they knew that Snow Black had a good heart. They were all dressed in fluorescent suits patterned with the Jamaican flag; they also wore black sunglasses to block out the blazing sun from their faces. As they arrived onto the fields, they placed the coffin down and proceeded with the service. They all comforted themselves with ital herbs so the pain of Snow Black's death wouldn't hurt so badly. Each of them paid a little tribute in her memory. After this a moment of silence was held as the song 'Three Little

Birds' by Bob Marley was played in the background. The Rastas sobbed and bawled to their hearts content, Big-bwoi blew his nose; loudly startling Pumpkin who was beside him. Yes, this was their moment of silence.

As the special service drew to a close, Snow Black's coffin was placed vertically, down onto a wooden platform on the ground; they had decided not to bury her properly, for such beauty should never be hidden away. They said their final goodbyes and farewells and off they all went, still in mourning.

"Noo! Noo! Mi cyaan leave she! Mi cyaan do it!" cried Dumplin.

"Cum on man, tap de cow bawling! Yuh hav no choice." Rum and Reggae had to drag Dumplin away from the scene as he was making an exhibition of himself.

A moment had passed, and it was not long after that a mighty, strapping black beauty had galloped into sight. Its exquisite long black hair shimmered in the sunlight as a handsome muscular young prince stepped off the horse. He stood fazed by Snow Black's beauty and hovered gently over her coffin. He had never seen someone so beautiful in all his days. His heartbeat accelerated as he drooled at her side.

"What a pretty gyal sah!"

Cautiously he opened the glass lid of the coffin. Completely dazzled and delighted he took hold of her body in his masculine biceps, holding it so close to his chest that his heart may have just skipped a beat, it was then that he kissed her lips passionately, savouring each second of the sensational, romantic taste. Snow Black instantly arose from her state of unconsciousness, their eyes locked intimately as they warmed each other's hearts smoothly with their gasping breaths of love and affection. It was, yes indeed, love at first sight.

"Oh so handsome! So…so…Oh, where hav u bin all mi life man?" Snow Black questioned devotedly. The prince chuckled casually at her question; he then drew her closer till there was not a single gap between them. Looking deep into her eyes as he held her hands against his chest, he asked fervently. "What is yuh name darlin'?"

"Snow Black."

"Snow Black yuh are mi true love, marry me?"
Astonished by such an unexpected proposal, all her dreams had suddenly started to unlock from the hidden places they once harboured. She had waited for this moment all her life and it was finally here, it was finally here.

"YES! YES! I WILL!" Her only reply could have been yes, and with that the prince took Snow Black's hand in his and as she arose from her coffin delicately, he held her in his arms with a firm grip as if he was never going to let her go.

Up from the distance came running the seven Rastas as they saw the moving figures from afar.

"SNOW BLACK! IT CAAN'T BE! YUH ALIVE! TANK DE LARD YUH ALIVE CHILD!" shrieked Ziggy.
They all flung their arms around her giving her the greatest loving hug. She hugged them back willingly whilst tear drops of joy streamed from her eyes.

"Tank yuh for every ting!"

"Wah yuh mean, oh no Snow Snow, yuh goin, oh why? Oh why?" whimpered Reggae.

"Yuh jus not too long cum bac from deh dead!" snuffled Pumpkin.

"Oh please stay!" pleaded Rum.
Her heart became overwhelmed with sadness and guilt

for the Rastas, as she knew that not even she really wanted to leave them either. She could never forget how kind and loving they were towards her. I mean how many people would take a complete stranger into their home, feed and nurture her? However, she knew she had a life to lead, beyond Yam-Yam Forest, and she wanted to see it for herself. She had been awaiting this moment her whole life and there was just no stopping her now, she was going to take it and run with it.

"Don't worry, mi never ever goin' to forget unu never, I promise, an I will cum bac an visit yuh all once mi sekkle." She gave them all one last hug, and kisses on the sides of their tearful, wet cheeks.

"We will miss yuh darling Snow Black," they waved and sobbed as she took her position on the back of the black beauty with her new husband to be.

"I will miss yuh too Ziggy, Reggae, Rum, Pumpkin, Dumplin, Tom-Tom and Big-Bwoi, an once agen, tank unu for everyting."

Off she galloped with her handsome prince. Far far away into a land and life of eternal happiness going to fulfil the destiny that awaited her.

# REALITY CHECK

As a child, did you watch all those children's films and cartoons about fantasy this and fantasy that? I know I certainly did. It seemed so fascinating, so exciting, and so real. However, as you grew older all that exciting fantasy life was suddenly burst like a big bubble into a basket of flames as you discovered that it was only a figment of your imagination. A shame really, I know.

I'm Jane by the way, Jane Pip. And do you want to know a little secret? Well do you? I don't think you're really, truly ready for what I'm about to reveal to you. Listen carefully and listen well, because information like this isn't commonly told. Fantasy Land is real! It's not just some silly old made-up stuff like grownups always describe it to be. It's real, I tell you, and I know exactly what you're thinking. Well, how would I know, right? I know because I've been there, there and back again, seen it all with my own two brown eyes and brought the t-shirt too. It's real!

Now obviously, I know that I can't just exclaim such a bizarre sounding fact and not even tell you the story, or else where would the proof be? Besides, without the story it's hard to even begin to imagine such a place.

I think you are very unaware of the incredible lifetime experience that you are about to embark on. I guarantee you; you'll have never heard anything like it. Once in a lifetime opportunity this is, and if I were you I wouldn't miss it for the world.

So may I suggest you sit back awhile, grab a blanket if needs be, maybe a biscuit or two and most importantly, enjoy…

**The story begins**

Jane Pip, not your average everyday ordinary teen, but more along the lines of a very 'unique' individual. She's a long bushy haired brunette, tall, with a slim-lined figure, big brown eyes that would never fail to misread a word on a page and glasses always worn on the tip of her pointy nose. Yep, she was pretty much different alright. She was never the sociable type, but would much prefer to spend her valuable time alone, *reading.* Yes, I said reading! Now I know what you're immediately thinking as a reader, but I tell you this, never be somewhat shocked that someone would rather choose to spend time engaging in words than with people, its perfectly *normal.*

On her way to school at a bright, early start of 8:00am, she was in a hurry to be first at the school library. Yes, I said library! Stop with the 21 questions now. Just before the 8:55am bell, the signal of another wonderful insight to more education in the world of Jane Pip, she wanted to refresh her mind full of words, phrases, complex, compound and simple sentences to alert and activate the brain before it was diluted with the noisome racket of school children.

The library, her personal sanctuary, was fairly large and bright, filled with books calling her left, right and centre to read them; most importantly it was *quiet* just the way she liked it. As she entered through the white double doors, the room automatically welcomed her presence as if it expected her. The librarians greeted her with the usual sharp grins and energetic waves as they did each morning, showing her the new stock they were about to have in, and giving her sneak preview copies before the rest of the school even had access to them. They favoured her greatly as they saw great potential in her character.

They had never seen a person with such enduring passionate enthusiasm to read. They had never met a student quite like her, not even remotely close which is why they were so fond and so keen to encourage her to always be herself, despite how odd and unsociable people thought she was. She resumed her usual place of comfort where she always sat to read, right in the corner of the library where she was hidden, hidden away from eyes, voices, and people. She was in a corner where she was able to think and imagine aloud without judgement; she was in a place where she could hide away from reality awhile. Her mind always liked to wander at every given opportunity into a place where only Jane could go, and that was her corner for doing this. She had brought along with her a pile of books, stacked high; she could be extremely indecisive from time to time. After some time, she had put several books aside; she was now down to a top 3. This included a non-fiction, a novel and a fiction book; they were all completely different, additionally with all of them looking considerably interesting. Finally, coming to a decision, she had made the biased decision that she was going to choose the book that she was going to read by sight and not by content. This instantly eliminated the novel and the non-fiction book, leaving the fiction book to remain. She was attracted to its resplendent covering, and ornate fonts that leaped excitedly from the page in rejoicing motion because Jane had picked it. Its title read. 'Fantasy', relevant to what Jane intended to do that very morning, fantasise. Turning the book to the back, she wanted to get an insight to what 'Fantasy' was about. Strangely, it contained one sentence reading, 'I think you are very unaware of the incredible life-time experience that you are about to embark on.' Jane found this very unusual as the blurb purposely failed to provide her with the information she was looking for. However, it was now 8:30am, *get Reading*, she thought, as she wanted to spend a good amount of time in 'Fantasy'.

Turning the thin, fragile page of paper, so easy to rip, she placed her glasses on the very edge of her nose to prepare her reading stance. The page contained a question in big bold writing.

# "Are you ready?"

Paying no mind, she turned to the next page, reading

**"There's no turning back from this point on, so if you answered 'yes' to the first question, turn to the next page."**

Turning to the next page, it read

# "I see you answered yes then, excellent choice, well I guess you're ready then."

Jane had become impatient with the books silly antics by now.

Turning to the next page, it read

# "On your marks"

then the next page

# "Get ready"

then the next page

# "Get Set"

then finally

# "GO!"

Nothing happened. What on Earth? Jane flicked through the rest of the book frustratingly, only to find blank, plain pages full of *nothing!* Was this some sort of practical joke, she couldn't help but wonder. Going back to the page that read **GO!'** she repeated it aloud in a confused tone, "**GO!**" she uttered.

"*AAAAAHHHHHHH!!!!*" The journey had begun.

She was blinded by the brightness; blinking her eyes harshly, she patted what felt like cushiony floor in search for her dependent glasses. Pausing for a moment, she'd sensed some sort of movement or footsteps coming from her left. In her hazy vision, a short, stubby figure appeared holding her glasses out for her to take hold of, she took them gratefully. Finally, blowing on them and wiping the frames clean with her school jumper sleeve she placed them back onto the place where they belonged. Looking up, she jerked back at the sight of seeing the most phenomenal looking thing she had ever seen in her life.
It was completely furry from head to toe, like a big teddy-bear it looked cuddly and cute; it had two fluffy legs, arms and eyes with purple long lashes.

It basically had similar features that a human-being contained. However, strangely it had no nose or ears.

"Me, Tippy-toe-toe!" the thing exclaimed with a squeaky high-sounding pitch.

Jane was mortified at the fact that something so weird could actually speak let alone sound the way it did.

"ME, TIPPY-TOE-TOE! ME, TIPPY-TOE-TOE! ME, TIPPY-TOE-TOE!"

Why was this thing shouting, Jane had heard it the first time, maybe it was repeating itself until Jane revealed her identity and told it what her name was.

"My name, I mean me, Jane Pip," she looked at it awkwardly with her head stretched back as if in resistance to get too close.

"You, Jane Pip, You, Jane Pippy-pip, You, Jane Pippy – pip-pip."

"No, Jane Pip is just fine thank you."

"NO! YOU JANE PIPPY-PIP-PIP! YOU JANE PIPPY-PIP-PIP! YOU JANE PIPPY-PIP-PIP!"

"Alright, alright, me Jane Pippy-pip-pip."

How in the world did I get here? And what am I doing? Jane wondered. Suddenly a light bulb appeared in her head, *The Book!* but how? she anticipated. With no more time to anticipate to herself, she sunk through her unsupportive cushiony rest position. To find herself surrounded with more extraordinary creatures that looked similar to the appearance of Tippy-toe-toe. They all spoke at once, rudely over one another, eager to introduce themselves to Jane. These things were too friendly for Jane's liking; remember, she was not the sociable type.

"Tippy-toe-toe, could you tell me where I am please?"

"Aww, Jane-Pippy-pip-pip, don't'ter worry'er you'er ar'er in'er 'Fiantasy Land'er!"

In an English translation, Tippy-toe-toe had just told Jane that she was in 'Fantasy Land'.

"I'm in WHAT?!" So it was true all along. It does exist; I wonder if this is where aliens come from, the Yeti, the Loch Ness Monster and all the other so-called mythical made-up creatures.

Tippy-toe-toe offered Jane a furry arm and helped her to her feet; she struggled to stand straight as the surface she stood on seemed to be moving. Looking beneath her she saw that she was no longer on the ground but floating in mid-fantasy air on top of a gigantic daisy. She couldn't believe her eyes; she never knew it was even possible for a flower to be so big; this was clearly unrealistic, she presumed. She dared not even look down, for she had a great phobia of heights and from what she could feel and see she was evidently high up. After a brief journey, she landed safely. Tippy-toe-toe zealously ushered her to go before him off the gigantic daisy. To keep him happy, she did as she was told. A sign hovered luminously ahead of them, with glowing lights that twinkled around it. It read 'THE FANTASY LAND TOUR ENTRANCE'. She stood dazed at how magnificently beautiful the sign was.

"Come on'er, come on'er Jane Pippy-pip-pip!" Honestly, Tippy-toe-toe was incredibly eager for Jane to explore his home land. Willingly she complied, and walked beyond the entrance sign into the 'Fantasy Land' tour.

One word, **WOW!** It was absolutely amazing. Indescribable. Unimaginably out of this world. You would have to see it, to believe it. Jane Pip had seen it all with her two brown eyes. She was living, seeing and breathing 'Fantasy'. It was as real as can be. The land was filled with chirpy sunshine in every visible sight. The land was filled with abnormal creatures of different shapes, colours and sizes; although it was hypothetically freaky, Jane was fascinated. The fantasy mid-air skies were filled with red-yellow clouds, pink-orange clouds, and green-white clouds, just floating out of any and every where. The most peculiar thing about them was these weren't just any ordinary colourful clouds; they were edible candyfloss clouds.

"Here'er you'er can'er eats it!" Tippy-toe-toe kindly handed Jane a chunk of candyfloss cloud. And this wasn't just any candyfloss; it was pink–orange candyfloss. It was the key to her heart, after reading of course. She ate it wasting not a morsel; licking her fingers repeatedly, she savoured the sweet aromatic taste that lingered on her taste buds.

"More floss-floss!" insisted Tippy-toe-toe.
Jane nodded assuredly, along came the gigantic daisy again.

"Now'er we'er move'er on'er, come'er, come'er Jane Pippy-pip-pip."

Suddenly there was an immediate change in atmosphere. The scenery was ravishing pink with a hint of strawberry flavouring. The daisy landed for Jane and Tippy-toe-toe to get off. Jane's eyes widened as she was surrounded by mammoth, scrumptious sweets! Bonbons, Opal fruits, Skittles, Refreshers, Wham bars, Fruity pops, Sherbet, Drumsticks, Mojos, Chewits, Love Hearts, Swizzles, Parma Violets, Ginormous of the Ginormas, Basset's Liquorice and it didn't stop there, that's all her eyes were able to see.

"WEE! WEE! WEE!" Tippy-toe-toe was having a blast, as he slid laughing hysterically at the top of his furry little lungs down a chocolate-fall of dairy milk chocolate into a swimming pool of it. Jane was astonishingly mesmerised at the large chocolate fountain fall, and even more delighted to see the pool of it beneath her. She was soon to follow Tippy-toe-toe's lead, by diving down the fountain fall into the chocolate pool of blissful ecstasy. That was funny, she'd lost sight of Tippy-toe-toe, and suddenly the heavy weight of a bonbon sweet ball smacked her headfirst, dazing her for a moment. It was Tippy-toe-toe clowning around.

"OI! YOU CHEEKY BUGGER!"

She then threw it back at him, missing terribly, and so on the game continued back and forth back and forth until the heavy bonbon sunk miserably underneath the chocolate pool.

"OH NO! bonbon gone'er, it gone'er!" Tippy-toe-toe wanted to carry on playing and was resistant to accept the fact that it was now over. Jane trod through the thick contents of dairy milk chocolate to get to where Tippy-toe-toe was. She comforted him is his time of disappointment. He buried his head in her skinny body, whimpering softly into the cotton fabric of her clothing.

"There there, Tippy," patting his furry body, she saw that the gigantic daisy had arrived to take them to another part of the tour. She carried, and I mean literally had to carry Tippy-toe-toe onto the daisy as he refused to walk. In the next breath Tippy-toe-toe was back to his normal self, well his behaviour wasn't exactly what humans would call *normal.* However, he was back to the 'normal' Tippy-toe-toe, doing what he did best, being loud, hyperactive and overexcited. Jane preferred him much more like this.

The gigantic daisy dropped them off onto the most ravishing green scenery, filled with a whole plant and animal kingdom. These weren't just any ordinary plants and animals; these were the plants and animals of

'Fantasy'. There were the most ludicrous looking sights she had ever come across, there were tigers with pig-feet, and she then assumed that no doubt it could be subjected to 'Swine'. There were birds with long, floppy rabbit ears, fish with frog legs, horses with fins, monkeys with hair, oh no! Wait a minute, that was normal, but the list goes on. Here comes the most exciting part, these animals and plants could TALK! It was ridiculously insane, talking animals slightly understandable, but a plant, that's something no human in their right minds of sanity could come to terms with, it, was just not realistic. Yet again, Jane was fascinated. She began making conversation with a purple tulip; it was giving her fashion tips on what not to wear. It also advised her to get rid of the hideous spectacles she called glasses and order the summer sale contacts on offer, half price at 'Plant Spec Savers'. The pig-footed Tiger gave her medical tips on how to act upon the various viruses and flu's going around, she was quite disgusted after hearing the amount of bacteria one is exposed to in one day. It reminded her never to touch any of the school door handles ever again. Tippy-toe-toe chased the floppy-eared birds around the luscious grass repeatedly scaring them so that they couldn't settle. To him it was just a game; I couldn't say that they were in the slightest amused by his torment. Jane called him as a distraction from the birds, Tippy-toe-toe then began chasing her. Round and round in circles until he exhausted himself. What a character? He was amazing. The gigantic daisy had arrived in no time again, it was very persistent and always on time.

The last part of the tour, the best part of the tour, fairy tales gone wrong. Jane met almost every fantasy character she had read about or watched as a child. She saw the three little wolfs and the big bad pig. They invited her for a cup of tea but could only provide cold water with it and no milk as the pig had blown all the houses down. She then met Lil Mizz Ghetto Red Riding Hood, she was a complete rebel, tattoo's, piercings, gel slapped down the side of her forehead with patterned squiggles, sovereigns on every finger, two thick silver chains, big gold hoops, a red hoodie, red baggy jeans and red Addi-colours. She was a straight barse! She taught Jane how to MC a couple 16's. She also met Snow Black and the seven Rastas who taught her how to dance 'Jamaican' style, Jane was whining up her little skinny body until her glasses fell off and as for Tippy-toe-toe he was on his head by the end of it. I suppose that's what Bob Marley's music does to you inside. Flabbergasted and drained, Jane and Tippy-toe-toe rested at a sleepover they were invited to for the night with Sleeping Beauty. She wasn't much fun, as she pretty much just slept, so Jane and Tippy-toe-toe made their own entertainment instead which was much better than sleeping. They had a MC'ing contest and a dancing contest, of course Tippy-toe-toe won with his energetic stamina to go on for hours on end. By the time he'd finished being in the limelight Jane was fast asleep.

The next morning, the gigantic daisy arrived for the final time. It dropped Jane and Tippy-toe-toe back to the entrance of the 'Fantasy Land' tour. Jane was surprised at how quickly it was all over, the creatures presented her with 'Fantasy Land' gifts of pink-orange candyfloss, a pig-footed tiger, and pictures of the characters in 'Fairy tales gone wrong'. Jane grew emotional, as the journey had been so adventurous and exciting. It brought a new light to her life that she had been waiting for and she wasn't ready for its spark to die. Poor Jane Pip. Tippy-toe-toe threw his furry arms around her neck choking the dear life out of her without realising.

"TIPPY! I CAN'T BREATH!" she yelled.

"Oh Jane Pippy-pip-pip you'er leave'er now'er," he bawled dramatically.

Jane once again comforted Tippy-toe-toe in his time of despair and once again, he buried his furry body into the cotton fabric of her clothing. At least this time she didn't have to carry him anywhere, thank goodness for that. Within the next breath Tippy-toe-toe bounced back to his *normal* self once again. She was used to his odd behaviour by now, as she walked towards the exit sign, she took one last look at the wonderful land of 'Fantasy' that she had experienced. Suddenly Tippy-toe-toe came leaping towards her in a boisterous manner. He placed a necklace round her neck gently; it was shaped in the form of a heart-star-moon it read 'Jane Pip came to Fantasy Land'. With a huge grin, she honoured the gift she was given and with that threw her arms around Tippy-toe-toe's furry neck. She held him tight not wanting to let go. He managed to wriggle free eventually, after tugging actively on her bushy hair. As she finally walked towards the exit sign once more, she turned and waved goodbye. She then exited; the exit was more exciting than the entrance. It was a massive wet slide leading to a humungous fuchsia bouncy castle, which bounced her straight back down to Earth. Back to reality.

# Friday 11<sup>th</sup> of February

Dear Diary,

   Can you believe it 3 DAYS until Valentine's Day and still I have no valentine! It's a joke. It was such a cliché for the last day of term today, people flashing their poxy cards around wondering who their secret admirers were. I bet they knew really, half of them probably sent them to themselves like I did. Sad I know, but I couldn't bear the embarrassment of all my friends having one apart from me. Amanda got 13 cards the lucky bugger! Lissy got 7 and Lasia got 3, I don't know how that one works, Lissy and Lasia are identical twins they practically look exactly alike if anything, strange that Lissy received more cards though. But who cares the point is I received 0, nought, zilch! It's so not fair.

  They were all blushing like big weenies asking me rhetorical questions such as "Who do you think it's from Mel?" Yeah, right like I'm really supposed to know the answer to that, what do they want me to do, take handwriting samples from each of the cards and do some sort of weird scientific investigation with them, in order to identify the culprits that wrote them! **Newsflash!** I do have a life, thanks.

  Should be much brighter spells tomorrow, Kieran Myers is having a Valentine's House Party, he's invited a majority of the year group including me, Mands, Liss and Lasi. **Newsflash** again! You would never guess who is going to be at that party too, OMG! OMG! I can't even say his name without having an epic. CHAD RILEY!! OMG! In my eyes he is the most gorgeous boy alive, Mands, Liss and Lasi don't see the big deal about him, but they need their eyes testing. They clearly have no taste when it comes to boys; I mean Mands had the hots for Petey Mackintosh! WOW. Now that's serious, bro! The thought of it makes me physically, emotionally, mentally and verbally SICK! He has major acne and his breath stinks of spearmint 24/7. Okay maybe it's not a bad thing, because one might argue that at least he has fresh breath, but every time we engage in a conversation that's all you can smell, it can make you feel quite sick after a while. But anyway back to the subject of Chad, I have to look super duper amazing tomorrow, if I want Chad to notice me. Well not notice me because obviously he has noticed me before, like that time in maths we both went to walk into the classroom at the same time, but him being the perfect gentlemen stopped and ushered me to go ahead before him, he smiled at me too when we took our seats. His smile's so dreamy; he has the most perfect white gleaming teeth. I wonder what toothpaste he uses, probably 'Colgate,' like me, and this time I want him to really notice me without being dressed in an ugly silly old school uniform. What to wear? What to wear? I really don't have a clue.

Oh well, not an issue, I'll just decide tomorrow when the girlies come over, for every event without fail our priorities are to help each other choose the perfect outfits. It's essential in a girl's life to have friends that actually care about their appearance so that they don't end up making a complete and utter clown out of themselves by looking like someone out of, I don't know, a 'Shrek' movie. However, don't get me wrong, I have quite a good eye when it comes to fashion and style, but the odd opinion or in my friend's case, approvals won't hurt.

Hang on; I'm sensing something looking over my shoulders.

"JOSH GET OUT!"

Sorry, little brothers. I think it's a sign, I'm going to hide you now Diary, I'll attend to you again tomorrow when intruding eyes are far away.


**Downstairs**


Partaking in my usual daily routine of having vanilla ice-cream with crushed digestives biscuits at precisely 5:37pm… Oh No! And the unfortunate events just kept on coming …

"DAD! MOM! WHAT ARE YOU DOING?" This question only required a limited response, why did I even bother to ask; you know what, there are some things you wish not to see, hear, smell or think in your

ONE precious life. I think parents are accountable for most of these unwanted experiences happening. It's so not cool. My parents were …. Wow, I'm so ashamed to even say this. My parents were kissing!

Oh gosh! I have no Valentine's, no secret admirers, no privacy (thanks to Josh), and I've just seen the worst sight ever, PARENTS KISSING! Eww yacky dum-dum! Yeah right, like my life couldn't get any worse!

## Back in my bedroom

Hmmm... Tossing and turning...hmmmmmm.

It's no use, I can't possibly sleep, not like this, I'm too excited. I can feel tomorrow already, feel the excitement circulating through my bones. As well as excitement I feel just slightly nervous too, I just want everything to run smoothly that's all, I just want to have a good time. One night for nothing to go wrong, nothing embarrassing to happen, just a beautiful, fun night.

## Saturday 12th of February

This is the day! It's here! It's here! OMG! It's actually here. I've brushed my teeth twice already this morning and rinsed thoroughly with 'Aqua Fresh' mouth wash for that extra refreshing minty taste. Eww! I'm having a Petey Mackintosh moment, oh heck no! I decide to have a fruit salad for breakfast, keep it healthy you know?

At 3:00pm I start getting ready, hair and make-up takes considerably long as I'm a perfectionist. Not too much in this case as it can sometimes look overpowering. Keep it light but nice I say.

By 4:00pm the girlies were round with a case full of clothes, how many outfits would they possibly need to decide from, one might question? Surely they *can't be* that indecisive, not even I am, and hello, I'm Queen Perfectionist! Lissi and Lasi are ready in 45 max with matching outfits on accident. It's so cute as they go out of their way to make sure they don't look the same. After half an hour of Lissi getting ready in the bathroom upstairs and Lasi getting ready in the toilet downstairs they both came in my room in matching outfits of denim jeggings and checkered blouses. The only difference was Lissy's blouse was checkered grey, yellow and white whereas as Lasia's was checkered pink, brown and green. They both refused to change to suit the other as they claimed that they both were in the outfit first.

Anyway next was Mands, she was always a toughie, she had no figure so we had to be careful what we made her wear even though she just stuffs anyway. She looked stunning after we'd finished with her though. Gosh, I'd wonder what she would do if we weren't there to guide her, she wore a purple pleated skirt with shiny black leggings, a pink-toned blouse and gladiator sandals coloured purple, yellow, pink and brown. Finally, it was my turn; I don't know why I'm always left until last. Well you know the saying 'Save the best until last,' and that's exactly what they were doing, because no doubt I was going to look the best tonight. After a long attentive time of making me an exquisite sight of perfection, I would say we all had produced a beautiful on point look for the party. I wore a sassy short black dress that complimented my long legs with a pair of knockout 3 inch black and silver heels. I was ready to go.

## At the party

Music pumped so loudly we could hear the speakers from down the street before we even came to Kieran's house, that's how we knew that we were at his house.

"I'*MMMMMMMMMMMMMMMMMMMMMMMMMM* COMING OUT! SO YOU BETTA GET THIS PARTAY STARTED!"

We all sang, shouting hideously out of tune at the top of our lungs, but we didn't give a care in the world. It was our night and we were going to make the most of it.

**Back in my bedroom**

Dear Diary,

　　　IT WAS AWFUL!!!

　　　AWFULLY AMAZING!!!! ☺

Everyone was there apart from CHAD! Well to begin with. I was more than disappointed at first, but I couldn't show it and give the girlies any satisfaction of saying the famous words of 'I told you so'. So I completely surprised them and had a blast! In fact I was in the middle of the dance floor most of the night dancing away like there was no tomorrow, I even did the karaoke four times. 'Puppy Love' definitely went the best, my heart and soul went into it along with the numerous sips of Archers I had throughout the night. Lissy had to take the bottle away from me at one point.

"I think that's enough for the night Mel," she told me. "Let's not lose our heads in Kieran Myer's house."

Oh, Boo Hoo Party Pooper! I told her that she wasn't my mother and if she wanted to be a granny for the night then she was more than welcome to, but I was going to have me some fun. After shouting my view and publicly humiliating my best friend, I then told her to leave off before running outside after feeling incredibly faint. The outdoor breeze comforted me in my time of disheartenment. My head sunk low into my forearms as I tried to take the mild pressure off my head; it was pounding my brain out! I tied my hair back just in case I was sick; I then, strangely, felt a hand on my shoulder.

"Lissy, I'm so sorry for shouting at you, I should have never have said all those things."

"Melanie, it's me," a deep, smooth tone replied.
Wait. That wasn't Lissy; I turned round casually trying not to display the fact that I actually felt a diabolical mess. My eyes froze immediately as a tall figure, with a brunette silky crew-cut hair style and rather large dimples imprinted cutely into the side of his tanned looking cheekbones, stood in front of me. It was CHAD!

I began fidgeting, stroking my palms and twitching, my stiff fingers paralysed from the cold. My knees became weak, so weak I stumbled, nearly falling to the ground. Chad grabbed hold of my arm helping me to keep my balance. As he did this, our eyes met for a moment, he smiled at me charmingly and I smiled back.

"Thank you."

"You're welcome, are you sure you're OK out here?"

"Err, erm yeah. Sure. I'm fine."
He raised his eyebrows, unconvinced by my response.

"You can't fool me Melanie Evans."

He knew my name! He knew my name! He knew my W H O L E name!

I couldn't exactly tell him that the reason why I had worked myself to an oblivion making an utter fool of myself was because I thought he wasn't going to be at the party. Otherwise how stupid would it have made me look, especially in the eyes of Chad. So I just told him that I wasn't feeling too well. I managed to convince him; we stayed outside the whole night just talking. One thing led to another and soon his arm ended up around my shoulder.

"MEL! So there you are," Mands just had to ruin the moment, she came hurrying out with Lissy and Lasia. They soon stopped short as they saw Chad beside me.

"I think I hear Petey calling me," Mands stalled in order to remove herself from the situation.

"Erm, I think I'll go with her," Lasia closely followed behind.

"Erm, I need to pee," and off Lissy went too.
Honestly, their excuses were so lame, they might as well have just said, "Heyy Chad, Mel is madly in love with you so we'll let her have all the time she can get with you!"

I think he got the picture of why my friends were behaving so strangely. I blushed a bit trying not to make eye contact with him for awhile. He just laughed.

"Your friends must erm, really want you to be out here with me."
I responded with a nervous chuckle.

"Hmm, you think?" I mumbled. The cold swept up my spine chillingly; I should have known better not to wear a dress in the month of February. Without even realising it my head somehow ended up on Chad's warm chest, my eyes closed a moment. Waking myself up instantly I tried to ensure that I didn't get too comfortable.

"Cold?" he questioned.

"Fr... Frr... Freezing!"

With that he took his jacket off, and placed it around me. It felt warm, soaked in the captivating fragrance of his aftershave.

"Why are you being so nice to me?"

He looked at me puzzled.

"Why can't I be nice to you, is it a crime?"

"No, but my question is why?"

He went silent, looking away.

"It's because...I think you're an amazing person Melanie Evans."

I choked on my own spit having a major coughing spasm; he patted my back harshly.

"Are you alright?"

"Yeah. Sure. Fine. I just thought you said that I'm amazing."

"I did."

I began choking again, he laughed at me whilst whacking me on the back several times.

I couldn't believe my ears, Chad thought I was amazing! He said it to my face. That I was amazing! For once in my life, I felt a sense of relief that I could just feel this way about a boy knowing that he felt the same way about me too. It was an awesome feeling just to endure for that moment in time.

It was 11:45pm before the girlies came back outside again, telling me that it was time to go before angry parents started yelling down mobile phones at them. Truthfully I knew they were right, but deep down I really didn't want to leave, I wanted to stay with Chad forever, I loved being in his company. He understood me; he knew how to make everything seem OK after what I thought would have been a night of complete disaster. He made me happy.

"Well I guess I have to get going then."

"Really, how you getting home? My Dad's comin' for me at 12:30 if you wanna lift?"

"No. No. I'll be fine; really, I don't live too far from here actually." He turned to Mands, Liss and Lasi. "You make sure she gets home safely." They frowned at him weirdly as if they couldn't believe that he was actually giving them orders for me, their best friend. He told me to keep his jacket. Aaah I know! I know! I'm using it as a blanket right now; I hope his fragrance doesn't fade.

As I turned to finally leave with a simple hug and goodbye, he called me back and asked if he could phone me sometime. We exchanged numbers and then bingo! That's when the moment of magic happened; Chad Riley kissed me full frontal on the lips. Overwhelmed and buzzing, I think I had definitely taken flight out of Earth's atmosphere. This was definitely the most PERFECT night everrrrrr!!!!!!!!!!!!!!. =)

## Sunday 13<sup>th</sup> of February

Dear Diary,

I can't stop thinking about last night. It was absolutely amazing. Mands phoned me this morning telling me that they had to carry me home, because I literally couldn't stand after Chad's kiss. I wasn't even slightly embarrassed about that funnily enough; I was too busy wishing that I could have re-lived that moment of me and Chad. Wow! It's like this isn't even real. Is this really happening to me?

"SOMEBODY PINCH ME!!!" …

"OW THAT ACTUALLY HURT! JOSH YOU STUPID LITTLE ANNOYING PESTILENCE! GET OUT! GET OUT! GET OUT! "

ARRRRRRRRRRRRGGGHHH, Little brothers! I swear I want to throttle him sometimes.

Back to Chad. I wonder when he's going to call me, do you think that maybe there's a chance that he will ask me out on Valentine's Day? Nah, who am I kidding, don't push your luck Mel. No, but he said that I'm amazing, so that means the chances are there's still a chance. He might, hopefully he will. Ooh, I'm just working myself into oblivion again. I think I need some rest; I didn't get much sleep last night. In fact, I didn't sleep a wink; I was too busy thinking about the party, and Chad and oooh how AMAZING it was. I can't stop talking about it, but I need to, I don't want to look like I've been waiting for this nearly half my secondary school life (which I have). I can't let Chad know this though, calm and casual Mel, calm, cool and casual. You must never show any signs of desperation, it can look so unattractive. OK, but seriously now, I'm going to sleep, I need to get my mind into a position where I can just stop thinking for a moment. I'm going to drive myself insane if I keep thinking about last night. OK I'm officially going to sleep now. Melanie Evans exits at 23:19 hours.

Night Diary

x

**Monday 14<sup>th</sup> of February 00:00**

Dear Diary,

AAAAAAAAAAAAAAAAAAHH!! GUESS WHAT!
GUESS WHAT! GUESS WHAT!

At precisely 00:00 hours, Chad Riley texted me,
Melanie Katie-May Evans saying and I quote "Will you
be my valentine?"

So that means you can officially call me Mrs. Chad
Riley ;) This is going to be the best Valentine's Day
ever, can't wait to tell the girlies.

Goodnight. Goodnight and Goodnight xxxxxxxxxxxxxx

## Day 1 – Left behind

THUD! It came bursting in as if it were in the 'Invincible Navy of the Spanish Armada' under the overall command of the 'Duke of Medina Sidonia 1588'. I hid behind my bedroom door quietly not uttering a word; neither a sound. I waited anxiously for its presence to stand before my eyes. The noisesome racket it made was like the sharp rifling pain of a stab wound to my ear. SMASH! BANG! CRASH! It showed no mercy. It charged the stairs; making an awful ear-splitting sound. I managed to catch this thing glimpsing left then right, then straight ahead. Straight at me.

Stepping back with a hesitant reaction, I thought it had seen me through the crack of the door. But no, it looked away and headed straight for somebody else's room. Adrenalin rushed, accelerated like a vast blow of blazing fire in a burning bush at an expeditious pace through my abdomen. I wanted to regurgitate the nauseous fear that had unleashed its presence throughout me. I watched in horror as the creature had once again forced its way through another area of my household in an inappropriate manner. This time it was another room. It was Rosie's turn. She screamed out a tremendous cry of apprehension as she was dragged carelessly out of her bedroom. I watched the abhorrent scene from behind a crack in the door.

"LET ME GO! LET ME GO!" was all that could be heard. These words penetrated through my mind as floods of tears swam consistently down my terror-stricken cheeks. I was a coward for not even venturing to help my sister, and I knew it. How could I have stood there and watched it all happen? My hands were clasped firmly over my ears to block out the heart wrenching sounds that she made. My eyes pointed above towards the heavens, as if begging for mercy upon her soul. I wanted it to stop. I just wanted it all to stop.

After a substantial amount of time, suddenly all was quiet. Too quiet. I couldn't hear Rosie anymore, or the ponderous, heavy footsteps of the mysterious creature. They had gone. Rosie had been stolen from me. She was the only thing I had left, she promised that we were in this together and that this creature would not be able to take on both of us when it returned. I hate promises, Rosie. I needed her; I was defenceless without her. Collapsing slowly back against the wall onto the bedroom floor, I was unable to function properly; I tried to make some sense of this situation. First Dad, then Mom, then Rosie, then…OH NO! NO! Yes, I had to face reality somehow; it was my turn next. The creature would be coming for me!

## Day 2 – Independence

Awoken by the sounds of violent winds smacking the faces of my double glazed windows, it was then that my independence began.

The house remained dead and silent, making me feel incredibly uncomfortable. The awkwardness of no house atmosphere was actually quite alarming as the only person who could create it was me. Everywhere I looked was a complete mess, the remains of what that creature had caused. Mom, who always liked a perfectly clean house wouldn't have stood for this. Not a chance. I tried to make the place look a bit more presentable, but then stopping myself, I had realised that there was no point in doing this as the creature would be returning very soon and be kidnapping me out of this dump-hole anyway. Negativity was the best possible solution in order to build up my bravery at this moment in time. Positiveness only weakened my strength.

Boredom had, without a doubt, filtered through my mind. Bedraggled by every rubbish reality show on the TV I gave up trying to entertain myself any longer. I was quite peckish, but I'm afraid cooking skills were not always my forté; I always depended on somebody else to do everything for me. Independence was draining, like CHEAP LABOUR! I was forced to do, think and provide for myself.

### 10 minutes later…
I gave my attention to a pile of old girly magazines that weren't even remotely interesting, none of them engaging not even a quarter of my undivided attention. *It was soo sad.*

### 5 minutes later …
Well, look on the bright side, I HAVE A FREE HOUSE FOR THE REST OF MY LIFE!
No, that wasn't fun. *It was soo sad.*
I was soo BORED! Seriously. I couldn't find anything to do. I practically had no life now. Seriously, *it was soo sad!*

### FINALLY!
I had found a constructive way to waste my time successfully. MUSIC!
I was going to blast music ☺

### 10 minutes later…
Bored again.

It was no fun singing by myself. It was usually me and Rosie singing silly songs out of tune and out of time at the very top of our lungs.

*0 seconds later ...*
The tears had started.

*0 seconds later ...*
And they kept on coming.

*0 seconds later ...*
I just couldn't stop!

Who was I kidding, the idea of me trying to be independent was just as stupid as the idea of a dog trying to walk on its hind legs.


**Day 3 – Going 'Mad'**

ENOUGH! IS ENOUGH! IS ENOUGH!
She scowled at me aggressively so I scowled back, with teeth displayed sharp as razors! I was completely astonished at the abnormality of my appearance. I did look an awful sight. So awful, I almost scared myself. My white cotton tank top was stained deeply in the orange mixed with yellow contents of my own sick. My stuffy nose was covered in nothing but mucus and the smell of dried spit from a sleepless night full of pain and sorrow. I was alone. Too alone. I was going mad in this place.

I hadn't eaten properly in the last 48 hours, apart from five full glasses of concentrated 'Smart Price' apple juice. I could see that I was losing ridiculous amounts of weight as I gazed at the blurred readings on the silver scales that I stood on. I threw it, like a mad woman on the loose, into the glass mirror in my bedroom. The glass shattered in rage of my actions, making a loud cracking exit into its death. I wanted to throw something else. It felt good. I went on throwing books, papers, old toys, boxes, just any object that made a good smashing sound when it landed.

"ARRRRRGHH and they said that vengeance will be MINE!" I snarled at my reflection in the murdered mirror whilst showcasing my teeth angrily like a wolf venturing for it's innocent prey. I looked so vicious; I looked so inhuman. Hyperventilating, I sat down on the cold, smooth floor. It made me slide repeatedly as I wasn't able to catch a grip with it properly.

"ARGGGGHHHH!! What the heck is wrong with me? I can't take this anymore! DAD! MOM! ROSIE! ANYBOODYY!!"

The exasperating feeling that had taken its hold over me was not about to win this battle. I had to keep it together; it was not the time for my inconvenient shenanigans. But no, why shouldn't I be angry? I've had to experience the burning fumes of serious hell these last 3 days! Why shouldn't I be allowed to be angry? Why can't I express the hurt of losing my immediate family? The people I counted on most to keep me safe from any form of harm or danger. Why should I contain myself? WHY?

*I was going Mad!*

*I needed help.*

*Somebody … Anybody … Please …*

*I was going Mad in this place!*

## Day 4 – A Sense of Hope

Awoken by the sounds of birds singing in harmonious symphony, that managed to swim lightly through the sunrayed faces of my windows. It was then that I had felt a sense of hope. I managed to grace the mirror with a smug smile, with half risen cheeks. Washed clean, and dressed in fresh, soap powdered smelling fabrics I could say I started to behave like a *normal* person again.

I treated myself to the scrumptious meal of a full English breakfast including all the trimmings. (I know, I actually cooked something!). Then to wash it all down I had a refreshing healthy glass of tropical fruit juice.

Sitting in the garden for an hour and a half I was in deep reflection with myself. It was rather interesting, although it does sound a tad insane. I found that being still and silent, helped me to get in touch with my inner self. You should try it.

I began to reflect on the importance of family and friends, its true what they say, 'You never realise how much you truly love someone until they are gone.' You want to know the really sad thing; I never had the opportunity to tell my family and friends how much I truly loved them before they were stolen from me. I suppose you strut around thinking that nothing bad will ever happen to anyone close to you. I suppose I always thought that I was exempt, hmm, strange that.

My Dad would always say to me 'Quit the pouting happy', this was his way of saying the Sun won't stand still for you.

Whenever I felt myself going through some sort of early mid-life teen crisis, Mom would always say 'If your bottom lip were any closer to the ground I could use it as a skipping rope, so how about you stretch it a bit with a smile.' ☺

As for Rosie, she was never really the word master; she liked to keep it simple, plain yet effective. Her solution to most problems was 'Life is too short for tears, so stop feeling sorry for yourself and get on with it!' (You can see why I never went to her for sympathy).

I had never appreciated any of these phrases until this moment, in fact when Dad, Mom and Rosie used to say all these things, I just used to think they were taking the mick, or in Rosie's case, just being mean. Now I knew that they only said all these things because they cared about me too much to allow me to be sad.

***0 seconds later …***
The tears had started again.

***0 seconds later …***
And they kept on coming again.

***0 seconds later …***
I just couldn't stop again!


## Day 5 – Still waiting…

The night was young and dominating. It had been approximately 4 weeks, 6 hours and 11 seconds since this still remaining anonymous creature had been out on the loose. It had captured many people. Many that I didn't know, and many that I did. Loved ones. Family. Friends. Why? was the question that still remained. I knew that I was bound to be next. It was coming for me, and there was nothing I could do. If I ran, it would only follow. If I hid, it would only seek me out.

I began packing away my most sacred possessions. Just in case. In case of my 'no return' then they would be hidden, safe from eyes and hands that would never be able to have the satisfaction of claiming them. It was a sad moment.

There was only one thing that was worse than danger itself, and that was waiting for it. It was too much to bear, still waiting. I scanned each area and every room of the house repeatedly, cherishing every single born memory that had ever once lived, happy, sad, and angry. It was a sad moment. I went in *every* single room, but *one. Rosie's room.* I just couldn't. I just couldn't bring myself to go in. I just couldn't do it. Intermittently I started to turn the door handle but then stopped sharply. But why was it so hard for me just to open the door and let myself in. It wasn't like the usual routine where I had to knock because Rosie was so prestigious and personal about people just barging into her room.

*Awkward Silence…*

I now knew the shameful truth as to why I couldn't bring myself to go in there. I knew why, I'll even tell you why. It's because of guilt. I felt guilty for letting my sister down. I looked her directly in the face as she was being taken, the fear in her crystal blue eyes, the tears of anguish and pain shortlastingly living on her cheeks a moment, to then dying on her lips. I watched in horror, whilst protecting my own self. As long as I was safe, Rosie didn't matter. Shame on me.

*What would you have done if you had been in my position?*

I finally let myself in; the floorboards creaked slowly as if in mourning for their owner. The room was cold and dead, creating quite an intense atmosphere. Something didn't feel right. I had been in Rosie's room many times, however I had never felt its atmosphere the way I did now. Its preternatural sense suffocated me until I felt breathless, trying to become ignorant to the abnormality of what was happening to me, I took a seat on the edge of Rosie's bed. Stroking the quilt cover softly, my hands sank deeply into the smooth enamelled fabric overlaid with the beautiful decorative covering of lilac butterflies. Observing the room with great speculation, I came across an unusual pile of what looked like photos. Picking them up I began flicking through them, to my surprise I had found undiscovered family pictures. I had never seen any of them before; I actually looked nice in the majority of them for a change too. Considering the fact that in my baby albums, in most of the images, I'm either pulling silly faces or not looking at the camera. I was never really a photogenic child.

My eyes had immediately frozen still as I came across a picture of me and Rosie. We were both wearing matching outfits of yellow dungarees, white frilly tops patterned with daises and silver jelly sandals. I began to laugh hysterically at how completely ridiculous we both looked, but then I began to look beyond the clothes and the silly pigtails and I saw a memory. A memory of happiness with *my sister. My Rosie.*

It was another sad moment, leaving Rosie's room I took one last look at it, as I knew I wouldn't be entering it again for the time being. *"I'm so sorry Rosie,"* I whispered gently as streams of silent tears ambushed my face. Returning to my room, I placed the family photos safely into the box where I had carefully laid the rest of my sacred possessions, I placed the picture of me and Rosie on top, taking one more moment to look at it, I then placed the cover over the box shutting it tightly.

*It was a sad moment.*

*Still Waiting…*


## Day 6 – It Was Time!

It was time. I felt it in the depth of my petrified flesh. I felt the blood circulating round my heart at lightning speed. It was time. No more waiting. No more. It was time. I closed my eyes in deep thought, thinking of all the bad things I had done throughout my life. But nothing, nothing I had done was so extreme for me to deserve such cruel and heartless punishment. But it was time. At approximately 23:00 hours, I remained silent, still waiting. ASLEEP!
**BANG!**
What was that?
**BANG!**
It was time.
# BANG!
  The door swung open with such mighty force that everything that once stood in place in the room was now scattered on the ground. And there it stood. The black figure. The anonymous thing!
I screamed, kicked and tried with great abundance in order to struggle away from its grip, it was firm and tight, leaving me no choice but to accept the situation for what it was. I felt emasculated from all strength in my bones, just an obsolete human being.
  In the open broad night light of the stars I felt the bitter wind as it smacked past my face, the criminal opened the

doors of its white vehicle that looked like a small death trap from what I could see. He flung me in the back seat carelessly, slamming the door with such aggression that I felt the vibrations through my chest. The seats were cold and damp, giving off a foul smell that made me incredibly nauseated. *Where was this thing taking me? What was it going to do with me? I wondered what it had done with Mom, Dad and Rosie?*

The figure then entered the car like a thief in the night; it started up the car immediately without even glimpsing back at me once. It drove at a wreckless speed, jilting me in the seat here there and everywhere.


## Still driving…

I felt a nervous wreck as I gripped my incisors firmly into my lips; I had never felt so close to death. Was this thing going to kill me? The tension was killing me enough. I just wished that things could go back to normal, my home, my family, my life. What was happening to it? Why was this happening to it? It just didn't make any sense. Why now? I just had no answers, left clueless and confused, there was just no justice.

The car had finally stopped and had arrived at its destination *safely.* Out of the white van got the reckless driver of a figure. *SILENCE.* Wham! swung the car door as it opened, the breeze that had entered with it was bitter and thick.

The figure stood in silence gazing through me with its agonizing stare. It then grabbed me by the ankles, hurling me in the most wreckless manner onto the hinge point of its broad shoulder blade. It was just a matter of time before my eyes were exposed to a pitch black atmosphere.

Unable to see, unable to feel, unable to touch, unable to adjust.


## Day 7 – Trapped

'Dear Lord', I cried …

If there was ever a time for me to believe in your existence, I would say that the most appropriate time would be now.

Please forgive me for all the bad things I have ever done throughout my life.

I'm even sorry for the time I called Demi 'smelly' Pitterswot a two-faced wanna be dumb blonde Barbie sell out!

I just pray that you speak to this creature's heart, let it free me, I don't want it to hurt me.

I just also pray that it hasn't hurt any of my family or friends.

Amen.


After praying for the first time ever in my life, I felt secure and at peace as if I was really heard. It just goes to show people's capability in their time of need.

But then I had to come back to reality at some point. There was an interminable silence that seized the dishevelled atmosphere. It was seemingly long and endless. The foreboding darkness abruptly sucked every sumptuous thing in sight like a malevolent vacuum cleaner, leaving nothing incongruous. Leaving nothing untidy. 76 hours, 3 minutes and 4 seconds, I had sat waiting. Waiting in this unfamiliar, dismayed place.

However, I refused to show any anxiety or fear or panic, although I still remained in complete perplexity as to where I was, and why exactly I was here.

My environment was haughty and violent. I scanned it with great accuracy having to encounter begrimed walls and a decrepit floor. As I looked up, I saw that the ceiling was worn and tatty. It was encompassed in damp mould which filled the air with a horrendous stench. A stench that was repulsing to inhale.

*What kind of mad being would live in such abominable conditions?*

A lustrous glimpse of foreign moonlight managed to glisten softly through a dainty crack in the wall. The alertness of its gaze distinctively focused on my face like yellow sun rays through a burning glass. It made me feel a sense of relief and hope, just like on 'Day 4'. To me this light was significant as it represented the light at the end of my dark tunnel.

The supercilious gaze of this daunting, obscure creature had taken its hold over me; sustaining utter focus as if in refusal to restrict it's attention from my sight. I felt the burning duplicity of his aura as his sinister, savaged pupils penetrated through mine. It brought about excessive sweat on my forehead like running water in a stream. I knew I was in danger. Alone and afraid. My body sat terribly uncomfortable in shape, as uninviting blows of constant chills submerged my pale skin with electrical impulses of consistent shivers. Backwards, then forwards I rocked hesitantly as if trying to bring myself to some sense of reality.

Bah, bum, THUD! Bah, bum, were the sounds of my heart as it pounded against the surface of my chest, in the sight of bloodcurdling tension.

I did everything in my willpower to defeat this overpowering feeling. I even began to reminisce about the freedom I once had, before being captured into this traumatic doom hole. I began to remember, distinctively, the days I sat waiting for this day to finally come to pass, and here it was. I hated it with a vengeance! I wish I had never been born to see this day. I just wanted to forget it all. Forget that I was even here, experiencing such horror. I wanted to block out the negative energy that violated me and suffocated me slowly.

I began to imagine the vivid imagery of a luxurious breeze appearing in the centre of my thoughts. It then swam gently through the air holes of my small, buttoned nose, whilst echoes of birds singing sweetly filled the drumming in my ears. I saw ravishing plantation swaying in a sensational motion as if dancing in rhythmic pace to its atmosphere whilst Mom, Dad, Rosie and I sat in a circle laughing harmoniously with one another. Just like I had remembered. It was explicit, exquisitely, delightfully…just a dream!

I regretfully re-opened my eyelids to revisit the grotesque appearance of my surroundings. My ears were then alerted to the disturbing sounds of heavy breathing. Disturbingly, it was not a sound being made by the unknown specimen. Panic-stricken I bit my lips intensely, as this strange sound appeared to be growing even louder. Looking in every possible direction, I was determined to distinguish where this sound was coming from. It had entwined itself into the open air with belligerent presence that vibrated vigorously against my body.

As it did this, the creature continued to unlock its glaring eyes from my sight. Its gaze grew more commanding along with the brutal sound. This made me emphatically vulnerable. I saw no way out. I was now at my wit's end and needed to be freed.

**I was trapped.**

I wondered what this psychopathic thing had done with my family and friends. Where it had disposed of them? Was I next to be disposed of? What was this thing going to do to me?
Who knew?
Only it knew.
However the situation at hand was, I still remained **trapped.**

*Glossary*

**A Dupey** - A ghost
**Badda** - Bother
**Caan/Cyaan** - Can/'t
**Dis** - This
**Dutty Wine** - A West Indian dance
**Er** -Her
**Farse** - Saying or doing something you have no business in
**Fi yuh** - For you
**Gwarn** - Go
**Im** - Him
**Ital Herbs** - Vegetation
**Jam** - Song
**Luk** - Look
**Mek** - Make
**Mi** - Me
**Pickney** - Child
**Sei** - See
**Sekkle** - Settle
**Shelly Belly** - A dance, named after a Jamaican dancer 'Shelly Belly'.
**Shud** - Should
**Tank yuh** - Thank you
**Tek** - Take
**The Bogle** - A dance, named after Jamaican dancehall star 'Mr. Bogle'
**The Butterfly** - A Jamaican dance move
**Tings** - Things
**Trow** - Throw
**Tu** - To
**Waan** - Want
**Wah** - What
**Wei yard** - Our house
**Whey mi deh?** - Where am I?
**Whu** - Who
**Widout** - Without
**Wud** - Would
**Yu**- You